"Don't you want to play?"

"I can't play with you," the white boy said.

"What's the matter, are you sick?"

"I just can't play with you any more."

"Why?"

"Because you're a nigger, that's why," the boy said.

My son did not cry, but in his eyes was the look of a wound, and I knew it would grow, become infected, and pump its poison to every tissue, to every brain cell!

ON BEING NEGRO IN AMERICA

A STARK, MOVING PORTRAIT OF INHUMANITY, OUTRAGE, AND DEFIANCE!

SAUNDERS REDDING is one of America's most superbly gifted Negro writers. The author of LONESOME ROAD and a number of other books on Negro history and culture, he is also a distinguished scholar and teacher.

ON BEING NEGRO IN AMERICA

☆☆☆☆☆☆☆☆☆☆☆☆☆☆☆☆☆☆☆☆☆☆☆☆

SAUNDERS REDDING

☆☆☆☆☆☆☆☆☆☆☆☆☆☆☆☆☆☆☆☆☆☆☆☆

*This low-priced Bantam Book
has been completely reset in a type face
designed for easy reading, and was printed
from new plates. It contains the complete
text of the original hard-cover edition.*
NOT ONE WORD HAS BEEN OMITTED.

ON BEING NEGRO IN AMERICA
*A Bantam Book / published by arrangement with
The Bobbs-Merrill Company, Inc.*

PRINTING HISTORY
*Bobbs-Merrill edition published September 1951
Charter edition published August 1962
Bantam edition published April 1964*

*Bantam Books are published by Bantam Books, Inc. Its trade-mark,
consisting of the words "Bantam Books" and the portrayal of a
bantam, is registered in the United States Patent Office and in other
countries. Marca Registrada. Printed in the United States of America. Bantam Books, Inc., 271 Madison Ave., New York 16, N. Y.*

WHEN CHARTER BOOKS DECIDED TO reissue Saunders Redding's famous little book in a paperback edition, the editors wrote to Mr. Redding at Hampton Institute, where he teaches English, to ask if he wished to update the book or perhaps write a new introduction. In due course an answer arrived from Nigeria, where Mr. Redding was then lecturing and traveling, telling them to go ahead with whatever updating they thought important to the text. The editors went over the book carefully. Some things, it was true, had changed: Mr. Redding was a little older, his sons had grown into young men, his father had died in 1961 at the age of ninety-two. Unfortunately, it was felt that, except for these things, no updating was needed.

That was early in 1962. Now, almost two years later and prior to the Bantam edition, we face the same problem with, alas, the same solution. Here, now in 1964, is *On Being Negro in America.*

"By the way, have I ever told you—"

"Enough of the truth?" she asked.

"There is never enough of the truth," the Colonel said. "There is only more and more."

—*From notes for*
  "The Colonel and His Lady."

ON BEING

NEGRO

IN AMERICA

1

THIS IS PERSONAL. I WOULD CALL IT A "document" except that the word has overtones of something official, vested and final. But I have been clothed with no authority to speak for others, and what I have to say can be final only for myself. I hasten to say this at the start, for I remember my anger at the effrontery of one who a few years ago undertook to speak for me and twelve million others. I concurred with practically nothing he said. This was not important in itself, but when one presumes to speak for me he must reflect my mind so accurately that I find no source of disagreement with him. To do this, he must be either a lack-brain parrot or a god. Though there are many lack-brains, historic and present circumstances prove that there are no gods dealing with the problem of race—or, as dangerous to the American ideal and as exhausting to individual Americans as it has been for three hundred years, it would have been settled long ago. Else the gods are singularly perverse.

There have been opportunities for complaisant gods. Every crisis has brought an opportunity. In Revolutionary times, even before we were a nation and the social structure and the ways of thinking that went with nationhood had solidified, there was splendid scope. But no gods arrived. Again, in the awful pause following the Civil War, when the social structure of half the country had disintegrated and men prayed only to be told what to think and do, no god answered. Instead, the ready devils of positive unreason took over and ruled for a long time. The First World War and the Second held the potential too, but we common men and the leaders we looked to were content with strong indictments and feeble measures. There was a hell-reek of baleful prophecy:

"A small group of Negro agitators and another small group of white rabble-rousers are pushing this country closer and closer to an interracial explosion which may make the race riots of the First World War and its aftermath seem mild by comparison. . . . Unless saner counsels prevail we may have the worst internal clashes since Reconstruction, with hundreds, if not thousands, killed and amicable race relations set back for decades." *

With such dire forebodings screaming in our ears, we fell back on a peculiar (and American) misinterpretation of Hegelian philosophy—that time, the flow of history, *inevitably* brings changes for the better.

* Virginius Dabney, "Nearer and Nearer the Precipice," *The Atlantic Monthly* (January 1943).

2

I SPEAK ONLY FOR MYSELF FOR AN-
other reason also. From adolescence to death there is
something very personal about being a Negro in
America. It is like having a second ego which is as
much the conscious subject of all experience as the
natural self. It is not what the psychologists call dual
personality. It is more complex and, I think, more
morbid than that. In the state of which I speak, one
receives two distinct impacts from certain experiences
and one undergoes two distinct reactions—the one
normal and intrinsic to the natural self; the other, entirely different but of equal force, a prodigy created
by the accumulated consciousness of Negroness.

An incident illustrates.

At the college in Louisville where I taught during
the depression, a white slum crawled to the western
edge of the campus. I could see its dirt, its poverty
and disease in any direction I cared to look from
my classroom window. In the littered back yards,
each with a pit toilet, snotty-nosed children with
rickets played and lank-haired women shrilled ob-
scenities at them all day long. I remember seeing a
man only once—an ancient, senile man bent with a
monstrous hernia. By the time autumn paled into
winter the pity I felt for the people in the slum had

been safely stacked away among other useless emotional lumber.

One day as I stood by the window thinking of other things, I gradually became aware of movement in the yard directly below me. The college building was as quiet as a church, for it was a Saturday when we had no classes. There would have been no shock in seeing a woman of the neighborhood dressed only in a ragged slip, but a powdery snow had fallen the night before and the day was bitter cold. When I saw the woman, who seemed quite young, she was lurching and staggering in the rear of the yard. A dog must have followed her out of the house, for one stood by the open door watching and flicking its tail dubiously. The woman's face was stiff and vacant, but in her efforts to walk her body and limbs jerked convulsively in progressive tremors. I could not tell whether she was drunk or sick as she floundered in the snow in the yard. Pity rose in me, but at the same time something else also—a gloating satisfaction that she was white. Sharply and concurrently felt, the two emotions were of equal strength, in perfect balance, and the corporeal I, fixed in a trance at the window, oscillated between them.

When she was within a few steps of the outhouse, the poor woman lurched violently and pitched face downward in the snow. Somehow utterly unable to move, I watched her convulsive struggles for several minutes. The dog came down the yard meanwhile, whining piteously, and walked stiff-legged around the white and almost naked body. The woman made a mess in the snow and then lay still.

Finally I turned irresolutely and went into the corridor. There was the entrance door and near it the telephone. I could have gone out and a few steps would have brought me to the yard where the woman lay and I could have tried to rouse someone or myself taken her into the house. I went to the telephone and called the police.

"There's a drunken woman lying in the back yard of a house on Eighth Street, seven-hundred block," I said.

"You say drunk? In her own yard? Then leave her lay."

"But there doesn't seem to be anyone there, and she may not be drunk."

"You said she was drunk," the voice said. "Now what's the story?" There was a pause. "And who're you anyway?"

"She could freeze to death," I said, and hung up. Thus I washed my hands of it.

The woman was still lying there and the dog sat quivering and whining near her when a lone policeman arrived almost an hour later. The next morning I read on a back page of the local paper that the woman, aged twenty-six, had died of exposure following an epileptic seizure suffered while alone.

One can wash his hands, but the smudges and scars on the psyche are different.

I offer no excuses for my part in this wretched episode. Excuses are unavailing. The experiences of my Negroness, in a section where such experiences have their utmost meaning in fear and degradation, canceled out humaneness. How many times have I heard Negroes mutter, when witness to some misfortune befallen a white person, "What the hell! He's white, isn't he?" What the exact psychological mechanism of this is, I cannot say, but certainly the frustration of human sympathy and kindness is a symptom of a dangerous trauma. Never having been white, I do not know whether Southern white people feel a similar reaction to Negroes, but, considering their acts and their words, it can hardly be judged otherwise. Actions speak for themselves; printed words not always.

5

For there is this about books on the "race question" (how weary one grows of the phrase!) by Southern whites: they have no detachment. They may seem to have. Within what has always seemed to me a questionable frame of reference, there may be brilliant exposition, analysis, interpretation, and even history. They may roar, as do the writings of David L. Cohn; they may purr lyrically and graciously in the manner of Archibald Rutledge and the late William Alexander Percy; they may remonstrate and apologize with unobtrusive erudition, as Virginius Dabney's and Hodding Carter's editorials do; or they may bristle with the flinty phraseology of Howard Odum's scholarship—but nearly all of them elaborate an argument that is certainly not derived from self-knowledge and that cannot be effective as an instrument of self-control.

The reasoning in them is very subtle, not to say metaphysical, and it runs like this: History is an imperative creative force (from Hegel again!) and man is its vassal. It is beyond the reach and the control of conscience and also beyond direction and prophecy. It created slavery, the southwestward migration, the Civil War, Ku-Kluxism. History does not conform to man's will; it compels conformity, and under this compulsion man and his society and his institutions are shaped into what they are and into what they become by categorical directives as potent as the word of God. History is above moral judgment and history's errors are beyond redress. Man's world is mechanistic.

This is not mere error; it, too, is symptomatic of a trauma all the more dangerous because this concept of history is what most Southern whites believe when they are being reasonable about the race question; when they are writing books about it, or talking quietly in their living rooms; or when they come together and "gladly agree to co-operate . . . in any *sound* program aimed at the improvement of race relations." This reasoning, at once defensive and defiant, expresses itself in clichés, which are the hardened arteries through which thought flows. "The white South is *inexorably* conditioned by cultural complexes." "In both the physical and cultural heritage of the South there are certain cumulative and tragic handicaps that represent *overpowering* factors in the situation." There are "legal and customary patterns of race relations in the South, whose *strength and age* we recognize." * The idealism of these people of good will is negated by the meanings of their own phrases.

The pattern of reason these phrases express has been the most influential factor in race relations for nearly a hundred years. And if Hodding Carter, one of the young Southern liberals, is representative ("The spirit [of which these stories are symbols] is harmless enough; a little pathetic perhaps, and naïve and provincial. Let alone, it will, of course, wear itself out some day. Not tomorrow or next year or the next year. But some day." *), it promises to remain so for another century.

And that thorny prospect brings me to yet another reason for the personal slant of this essay. I do not wish to live with the race problem for the next one hundred years—though of course I shall not live so long. I do not wish to die knowing that my children and theirs to the third generation must live with it. I have known it too long and too intimately already. It has itself been an imperative, channelizing more of my energies than I wished to spare through the narrow gorge of race interest. Yet I have felt myself in no sense a crusader. I have not been uplifted with the compensatory afflatus of the inspired leader. Let me

* From the *Atlanta Manifesto* issued by white Southern citizens in 1944. Italics mine.

* From *Southern Legacy.*

be quite frank. I have done what I have, not because I wanted to, but because, driven by a daemonic force, I had to. The necessity has always been a galling affliction to me and the root of my personal grievance with American life. This should not be hard to understand.

Connected with all this, of course, has been a sense of impersonal obligation which I like to think of as growing out of a decent regard for the common welfare. This civic sense has not expressed itself widely in group and racial activities and organizations, for I am not that kind of person. If it is a fault, I am sorry for it. I tried to be that kind of person. At one time or another I have been a member of most of the racial uplift groups, and am still a member of some, and when I was in my early twenties I thought I had taken fire from the mass and that if need be I could exhort and harangue and make public protest with the best of them. But I did not know myself so well then. What I felt was merely the exuberant, youthful need for self-losing identification. It gives me sad amusement to recall that in those days a friend of mine used teasingly to call me "Marcus Garvey"—a name that was the very apotheosis of blatant race chauvinism. But I had no real chance to be blatant—a habit, I suppose, like any other—and no natural inclination. Nor could I really lose myself in the mass.

3

BUT THE YEARS OF MY TWENTIES were enkindling and tumultuous. The world was well into that series of social revolutions which started, we are told, with the First World War and is not yet ended, and the American Negro people were a kind of revolutionary catalytic agent in their own country. It was their historic role, to be sure, but it had been suspended while Negroes played a supernumerary part in the European conflict. Americans in general seemed not to realize what had happened in Europe. They did not think of it as change. It was merely an eruption which they had helped put down and were intent on sealing off with the cement of isolationism. But after the war American Negroes re-enlivened the spirit of revolt, and the country was alarmed by the truculent persistence with which they fought for the Dyer Anti-Lynching Bill, for instance, and by the vigor of their opposition to the confirmation of Judge John Parker to the United States Supreme Court, and by the inroads of Communism among them, and by their implacable solidarity in the Scottsboro case.

How emotional the times were! What comings-together, what incitement! Out of college just three years at the time of the Scottsboro case in 1931, I remember the almost weekly meetings. Especially do I remember one at which Alice Dunbar Nelson spoke.

The widow of Paul Dunbar, a Negro poet nationally famous at the turn of the century, Mrs. Nelson had been one of my teachers in high school and an old family friend. She was beautiful—tall, with ivory skin and a head of glinting red-gold hair—and she was also of great and irresistible charm. One thought of her as being saturated in a serene culture, even in divinity. I doubt that she had ever been much concerned with the common run of Negroes, and that night as she spoke to a large audience of all classes of a united people, she was like a goddess come to earth —but a goddess. In the end, with tears glistening in her eyes, she stretched out her gloved hands and cried, "Thank God for the Scottsboro case! It has brought us together."

It was a thing to arouse even one constitutionally insensible to mass excitement, and I was not insensible—not in those days. I had found that out the year before, my second in the deep South. A student of mine was murdered, apparently in cold blood, by a white man or men. It happened in the late afternoon, in a section of Atlanta some distance from the college, and I knew nothing of it for several hours. But that night a colleague of about my own age rushed into my dormitory room without the usual courtesy of knocking.

"Come on," he said, gesturing vehemently, "we got to go."

I resented his bursting in on me. We did not particularly care for each other anyway. "You might have knocked," I said.

"For Christ's sake, this is no time for the amenities!" he said. "We got to go."

"Go where? I'm not going anywhere."

"To the meeting."

"What meeting?"

"My God, man, don't you know that Dennis Hubert's been lynched?" His eyes blazed like fires in a draft. He was greatly agitated.

"What!" It must have been a yawp of horror and disbelief. The boy had sat in my class not five hours before.

"Lynched by some goddamned drunken crackers. The Negroes out in East Atlanta are getting together, and we're going to get together too. We're not going to take this lying down. Those crackers might come out here any time."

I could not follow his thinking, even after he reminded me that a relative—either an uncle or a cousin—of the murdered boy was on the college faculty; but the dangerous possibilities of "those crackers" coming bloomed in my imagination like poisonous flowers.

"And if they come, then what?" I said.

"That's what we're having the meeting for. Come on."

And I went. We were only a few, mostly younger instructors, and we tried to appear disciplined and resolute, but hysteria was abroad, and I was caught up in it long enough to pledge to buy a gun through the underground means we had to employ; and long enough to be thrilled by the possession of it when it was delivered in great secrecy the next day; and even long enough to wish to use it on any skulking white man that offered.

The college environs and, I suppose, all the Negro sections of the city, were like alerted camps. There were many false alarms: cars loaded with white men were prowling the neighborhood; another student had been murdered; some white youths had caught a Negro girl coming from work, stripped her of her clothes and chased her naked through the downtown streets. And to match these were the heroics, like guarding the house of the college president and of the

Hubert relative who was on the faculty. Every few days for a month Negroes held meetings, but after a time I did not go to them any more. They came to seem like public displays of very private emotions, in the same unbecoming taste of those obscene religious services in which worshipers handle snakes.

One day I took my gun and the box of bullets that came with it and rode out into the country and fired at a dead tree. Wrapped in greased, gray flannel in a cardboard box, the gun is still somewhere among my possessions, but I have not seen it since.

4

MANY NEGROES WILL DENY THAT THE force which I have described as daemonic has operated in their lives. If asked about it, they will take quick offense, as if it were of the same stripe as an unnatural sex drive which, of course, is wisely kept secret by those who possess it. They will aver that they live *normal, natural, wholesome* lives, even in the South. They will point out their "normal" interests in their professional lives and in their home lives. They will tick off the list of their white friends. They will say, truthfully enough, "Oh, there are ways to avoid prejudice and segregation." I have no quarrel with them (nor with any others): it is simply that I do not believe them. Having to avoid prejudice and segregation is itself unwholesome, and the constant doing of it is skating very close to a psychopathic edge. My experience has been that no two or three Negroes ever come together for anything—even so unracial a thing as, say, a Christmas party—but that the principal subject of conversation is race. One grows mortally sick of it.

So in a sense, partly through the writing of this essay, I seek a purge, a catharsis, wholeness—as all of us do perhaps unconsciously in one way or another. I do this consciously, feeling that I owe it to myself. I need to do it for spiritual reasons, as others need to seek God. Indeed, this is a kind of god-seeking, or at least an exorcism. To observe one's own feelings, fears, doubts, ambitions, hates; to understand their beginnings and weigh them is to control them and to destroy their dominance. By setting certain things down, I hope to get rid of something that is unhealthy in me (that is perhaps unhealthy in most Americans) and so face the future with some tranquillity.

Also, and finally, I hope this piece will stand as the epilogue to whatever contribution I have made to the "literature of race." I want to get on to other things. I do not know whether I can make this clear, but the obligations imposed by race on the average educated or talented Negro (if this sounds immodest, it must) are vast and become at last onerous. I am tired of giving up my creative initiative to these demands. I think I am not alone. I once heard a world-famous singer say that as beautiful as the spirituals are and as great a challenge as they present to her artistry, she was weary of the obligation of finding a place for them in every program, "as if they were theme music" wholly identifying her. She was tired of trying to promote in others and of keeping alive in herself a race pride that had become disingenuous and peculiar. The spirituals belong to the world, she said, and "yet I'm expected to sing them as if they belong only to me and other Negroes and as if I believe my talent is most rewardingly and truly fulfilled in singing them, and I just don't think it necessarily is." As a matter of fact, she added, she was having more and more trouble *feeling* her way into them.

I knew what she meant. She could no longer be arrested in ethnocentric coils: she did not wish to be. The human spirit is bigger than that.

The specialization of the senses and talent and learning (more than three fourths of the Negro Ph.D.'s have done their doctoral dissertations on some subject pertaining to the Negro!) that is expected of Negroes by other members of their race and by whites is tragic and vicious and divisive. I am tired of trying, in deference to this expectation, to feel my way into the particularities of response and reaction that are supposed to be exclusively "Negro." I am tired of the unnatural obligation of converting such talent and learning as I have into specialized instruments for the promotion of a false concept called "race." This extended essay, then, is probably my last public comment on the so-called American race problem.

5

Names have been given to the advocates and promoters of various racial policies. There are gradualists (and they are black and white), who feel that somehow by a process of mechanical progression everything will work out, though to what concrete ends they do not say. The race chauvinists advocate a self-sustaining Negro economic, social and cultural island, and seem to have no fear of a destructive typhoon roaring in from the surrounding sea of the white world. The educationists believe that intellectual competence as indicated by the number of Negro Phi Beta Kappas, doctors of philosophy and various experts will win for the race the respect it does not now receive. There are the individualists who urge that each man work out for himself the compromises that will bring the self-fulfillment he seeks. Finally there are the radicals (there are no degrees of radicalism among them) who, because they seem to see destruction as an end and would first uproot everything, are actually nihilists.

Various racial and biracial institutions look on themselves as representing and implementing one or the other of these policies. The Southern Regional Council, for instance, is gradualist. The Negro press is chauvinist. Most Negro Greek-letter organizations (of which there are seven national and many dozen sectional and local) are educationist. Howard University—though not its president—and the best-known private Negro colleges are individualistic in their approach. Until its demise, the National Negro Congress was radical.

But none of these is seamless, pure and undefiled. Into each of them have seeped influences from one or more of the others. In so far as the Southern Regional Council believes in segregation (and that is very far indeed), it is chauvinistic, and in as much as it sets a premium on intellectual growth as measured by scholarly achievement, it is also educationistic. By the very circumstances of their founding, private Negro colleges lean toward chauvinism, and they encourage this tendency further by courses in "Negro" history, art, literature, business and life. Recently, moreover, some Negro colleges have spoken in favor of the South's segregated regional education plan —the private ones for reasons not quite clear; the public ones because only segregation will save them from extinction. The radicals who, anyway, take the position that radicalism is the highest, brightest star in the ideological heavens, are very proud of the intellectual caliber of Paul Robeson, Ben Davis, and that other Davis, John, erstwhile president of the National Negro Congress. The Negro press, of course, reflects these conflicts and inconsistencies.

But something more fundamental than the contradictions accounts for the failures of these policies. Gradualism, a habit of thought that marks interracial activities in the South, is geared to the historic-compulsion idea mentioned earlier. It is mostly faith without works, thunder without God, and lengthy, frequently fraudulent reports of "victories" as represented in the decline of lynching and the "long step forward" (nearly a generation in the taking) from the

17

Holcutt case (1932) to the Swett case (1950).* As a principle, gradualism is very flattering to the Negro people. It ascribes to them superhuman patience, fortitude and humility in the face of very great social evils. Gradualism is *laissez faire*—a proscription of planning and foresight in the dynamics of society.

Chauvinism is as impractical for the Negro in America as it is fundamentally dangerous for any people anywhere. Even if Negroes could duplicate the social and economic machinery—and I doubt that they could—the material resources on which their racial island must then depend would have to come from somewhere outside. In a constantly shrinking world, complete independence and isolation are impossible. And even if they were not impossible for the Negro in America, would not the achieving of them result in permanent relegation to secondary status? The very numbers involved—that is, the population ratio—would assure it. I cannot imagine the white majority saying, "Sure, come on and set up your self-sustaining household in a corner of my house."

There is still a great deal of race chauvinism, and the fact should surprise no one. Negro organs of expression, including scholarly journals, document it: *Phylon: [A] Review of Race & Culture,* published by Atlanta University; the *Journal of Negro Education,* published by Howard University; the *Journal of Negro Higher Education,* published by Johnson C. Smith University; the *Journal of Negro History,* published by the Association for the Study of Negro Life and History; and a spate of lesser publications. A purely emotional conviction informs chauvinism. It is partly the frustrated pride that is expressed in "Negro History Week" observances, which dichoto-

* The courts denied Holcutt, a North Carolina Negro, the right to enroll in the State University. The course upheld Swett's suit for the same right in Texas.

mize United States history, and in courses in "Negro" literature and art, which turn out to be valiant but thin trickles forcibly and ingenuously diverted from the main stream of American life. Chauvinism springs from a natural desire to find remission from the unequal struggle between black and white, and surcease of discrimination.

The philosophy of the educationist is only superficially different from that of the individualist. The concepts in which they are hallowed seem only to obscure the fact that no man is completely the master of his fate. Only the immature fail to recognize that individual wishes now have almost no authority in the world. Educationists and individualists acknowledge the existence of co-operative evils but deny the necessity to act co-operatively against them. This is also, it seems to me, a denial of brotherhood—a principle which must be made to operate in increasingly wider and wider arcs of human endeavor. Any statement of the individualist's ideals would sound like a throwback to the time before theories of social compact, or better, social contract, evolved.

The contradictions and conflicts in all this go deeper, much deeper than any short and general analysis can indicate. They plunge their iron tentacles into the minds of individual Negroes, raggedly fragmenting them, scoring them into oversensitized compartments. It is this that we must understand when we think, for instance, of Paul Robeson; and when we hear a Negro college president declare himself opposed to segregation, while at the same time he urges the state to add graduate courses to his already substandard curriculum, so that Negro aspirants to graduate degrees will not embarrass the state's white university; and when we read on page one of a Negro paper a vilification of white women who "run after" Negro men and on the next page an encomium of a successful mixed marriage. This is more than simply resiliency and accommodation, and there is more than just Negro heart and mind involved. For the Negro is not *the* problem *in toto*, nor a problem *in vacuo*. His behavior, the patterns of his multiple personality, the ebb and flow of action and counteraction and the agonizing ruptures in his group life result from the ill-usage to which he is subject at the hands of American white people.

6

———

Looking back now, I know that the essence of these conflicts was distilled in my own boyhood home. My mother, who certainly would not have phrased it so, or even consciously thought it so, was an individualist. She was also the perfect embodiment of a type of Negro womanhood whose existence is still denied by those who cling to the old abasing habits of thought. Virtuous, educated and noted for her beauty, she lived her short life in a firm belief that the moral exercise of individual initiative, imagination and will was enough to overcome the handicap of a colored skin. I have before me now some lines she wrote, obviously thinking of her sons.

> And so you are a son of darker hue!
> Think then that God sees in your face
> A lesser image of his love and grace—
> The ills of life all meant for you?
> What light before you beckoning?
> The iron will, the open heart and mind,
> The hope, the wish, the thought refined—
> These compass points for a true reckoning.

These are not a full expression of her thought, for there was enough of the chauvinist and enough of the sense of reality in her to make it clear that in her time, except in the most unusual circumstances, the limits of progress for the Negro were within the Negro world. Yet she spoke with pensive pride of Howard Drew, who had been a great college athlete and who was then a Hartford lawyer with an entirely white clientele; and of Maria Baldwin, the Negro principal of the very estimable Agassiz School in Cambridge, where many Harvard professors sent their children; and of Lillian Evans (Madame Evanti), who sang opera for a season at La Scala; and even (though with less pride, for the theater was still suspect in her mind) of Bert Williams.

But my father was different. He took pride in such successes too, but it irritated him that the knowledge of them was not more widespread. He would have used them on the one hand as arguments against the white-superiority theories of Lothrop Stoddard, Madison Grant and Jerome Dowd, and on the other, as arguments for his own theory that the Negro could and should develop his own American culture. I saw him brought to the verge of tears when the Brown and Stevens Bank—"the richest and safest Negro bank in the world"—failed back in the early 1920's. And this was not because he lost money in that disastrous collapse—he didn't—but because that failure cast dark shadows over the prospects of a self-sustaining Negro culture. He saw other shadows many times, but he remained (and now in his eighty-second year remains still in his heart, I think) a race chauvinist. For him there was no incongruity between this and his insistence that his sons go East to a New England college.

Through all the years of my boyhood, my father was secretary of the Wilmington, Delaware, branch of the National Association for the Advancement of Colored People; secretary-treasurer of the Sara Ann White Home (now the Layton Home) for Aged Colored People; and a member of the board of the local

Negro Y.M.C.A., which he helped found. Besides, he had certain pet, private projects, like needling the truant officer for not making colored children go to school, and upbraiding the police for permitting (interracial) vice to flourish in some Negro neighborhoods, and scolding fallen Negro women and derelict Negro men wherever he found them. He was buoyant and earnest and uplifted in the prosecution of these activities. What characters were drawn to our house! How desperate they were (I know now) in their search for simplification and for that dignity of being that derives only from a sense of belonging!

For these—simplicity and dignity—after all are the true things for which men strive. Unable to attain them in the large sense, men slice life up into manipulatable segments, institute policies of control, reduce to some petty enslaving program and to slogans the great purposes of life—"America for Americans," "For the Advancement of Colored People," "The True Church"—and march uneasily toward their graves under the illusion that the particular distortion into which they have been drawn is the straight and narrow path to salvation.

My father was like that. I think that all the Negroes I knew in my childhood were like that. It was not altogether their fault. It need not be pointed out that they had almost no say in determining the basic conditions under which they lived, and that it was this common suffering that drew them together in the first place. But subject to the common suffering was no mass man, but classes and individuals, and what they endured together they examined separately in the powerful lights of personal and class interests and ambitions. And under these lights the caste principle, which white society insisted on and to which the Negroes were responding in the first place—under these lights, the caste principle broke down. Negroness was not itself enough. The phrase, "We're all Negroes together," so often heard as a battle cry, had only a sporadic potency. Within the Negro group there were bitter conflicts and grave contradictions.

I remember when the tidal wave of Garveyism °swept over the walls my father had been hastily building against it. He had not had much warning. As secretary of the Wilmington, Delaware, N.A.A.C.P., he read—nay, studied—the *Crisis*, the Association's national organ. He knew the official line was that Marcus Garvey was a mountebank and his outfit swindlers preying on the poverty and ignorance of the lower classes. "Do not," the *Crisis* said, "invest in the conquest of Africa. Do not take desperate chances in flighty dreams." My father knew also, with increasing disquiet, how fast the Garvey following was growing. But somehow he felt that only people of the slums *could* be attracted to it, and he did not think of Wilmington as having a real slum. Of course he was naïf in this, for a stone's throw east of our house began a noisome squalor of existence that spread like thick slime to the river. When a sturdy, hard-working citizen (respected because he was hard-working and kept his children in school and did not let his insurance lapse) came bringing my father an official invitation to join the Garveyite "line of march," my father issued an urgent call to the members of the N.A.A.C.P. for a meeting.

But it was too late, for suddenly the Garveyites were upon us. They came with much shouting and blare of bugles and a forest of flags—a black star centered in a red field. They made speeches in the vacant lot where carnivals used to spread their tents. They had a huge, colorful parade, and young women, tensely sober of mien and plain even in their uniforms, distributed millions of streamers bearing the slogan "Back to

° Marcus Garvey was a West Indian Negro who aroused a considerable interest, and organized a great following, back in the 1920's, around the slogan "Back to Africa."

Africa." My father and I stood on the cross street below our house and watched the parade swagger by. Among the marchers my father spotted more than one "Advancer" (his term), even their wives and children. They were not people of the slums. They were men with small struggling clothes-pressing shops and restaurants, personal servants, and what Thomas J. Woofter, Jr., calls "black yeomen," unlearned but percipient. They had been dependable attendants at meetings promising Negro uplift, and loyal though perhaps somewhat awed members of the N.A.A.C.P. Some of them my father had personally recruited, and low groans of dismay escaped him when he saw them in the line of march. I was a boy, but I remember. And not so much because of the parade as for what happened after.

For the coming of the Garveyites shattered the defensive bulwark around the protective community of Negroes. The whites did not understand this at first, nor ever fully. Accustomed as they were to thinking of the Negro as an undifferentiated caste, they could not be expected to. Where there had seemed to be solidarity, there were factions. Where there had been one leadership, now there were more. Where it had been common to associate the force in the local Negro world with individuals, now the mass seemed to rear up faceless; and where no spontaneous drive had seemed to exist, now there was a hum of self-generating energy. The whites did not understand, but some of them found and took an advantage.

In our district which, with only a scattered thirty per cent of the population white, was fast becoming a ghetto, Negroes had enjoyed political control. They had had no trouble electing one of their own to the school board and another to the city council. The same men had been returned to office time and again. What they did there (and they did little) seemed not nearly so important as just being there. They had enormous prestige and influence among Negroes, and they had not had to fight to keep it.

But in the fall elections of that year they did. Directed by agents from New York, the local Garveyites put up their own candidates, chosen on class lines: the encumbents who, in the common phrase, were "dickties," found their following split. The campaign smelled of pitch and brimstone and led to street brawls between the sadly outnumbered teen-aged children of the encumbent faction and the Garveyites. Still the whites understood only enough of what was happening to give it burlesque treatment in the press. But the agents from New York were professionals, and their professionalism soon showed itself. They made a deal with the white leaders in the ward. Before the Negroes knew anything, the whites had picked their own candidates, and while Negroes fought one another, whites won the offices.

This was a blow—but that is to put it mildly. In our town, as elsewhere in border state and northerly towns, the pattern of a strong, single Negro leadership was fixed (and so, I suspect, was the pattern of a strong, single Polish and Italian and Jewish leadership), and now the white people were in a quandary. The pattern had been broken; they themselves had knocked down the stanchion that gave stability to race relations. A bond issue was coming up, and Negro backing was indispensable to its success. Hitherto the white people had influenced the direction of Negro thought through local Negro leaders. But who were the leaders now? The white people needed them; they felt uncomfortable and even frightened without them; they needed to know and to control, if possible, what the Negroes were thinking. The race riots in Northern cities—Washington, Chester, Chicago —were still green in memory, and Wilmington itself had almost plunged into that civic horror. Congress just then was drumming up a Bolshevist scare, and

Congressman James Byrnes, of South Carolina, had called for indictments for sedition against certain national Negro spokesmen.°

But the Negroes were equally lost and frightened by the immutable evidence of their own factionalism —and frightened the more that white people knew of it. So long as they could seem to maintain a solid front, no matter what internal tensions actually rived them, they felt reasonably safe. But "Now the white people can cut us up," my father said. "We are divided." It never occurred to him that the last thing in the world the white people wanted was a divided Negro population. Enforced segregation and the caste system were proof that they did not. My father, who had spent more than two thirds of his life above the Mason-Dixon line, hated segregation, but he had developed the ghetto-mind which made it bearable and safe.

A war of impulses was (and is, I fear) going on all the time in both whites and Negroes. It is the symptom of an American psychological malady. It is also an indictment of our culture and an offense against democracy. Many understand this now, but most do not. Indeed, most have built sophistic bulwarks against understanding. They do not know this, for the many small, subtle fallacies which they abide through force of habit lessen their sense of moral conflict when they are faced with the great contradiction. My father's saying, "Don't ever trust a white man," is in intent no different from the white man's saying, "All niggers look alike to me." The phrases represent the lowest common denominator in the American race-experience. They are the essence of empiricism. They voice experiences so debased and so bereft of humaneness as utterly to discredit our way of life in the eyes of the world. They deny the

° See his speech to Congress on August 24, 1919.

inspiring first principle of democracy—that the person counts as person, no matter what his color or creed.

"Son," my father said, the night before I went East to college, "remember you're a Negro. You'll have to do twice as much twice better than your classmates. Before you act, think how what you do may reflect on other Negroes. Those white people will be judging the race by you. Don't let the race down, son."

I have no memory of protesting this terrible burden laid on my mind and heart. Indeed, I am sure I did not. What my father said checked with what I had been taught to *feel*. My father went on.

"Out East you may feel it less because there're fewer Negroes, or for the same reason, you may feel it more. Some say one thing, some the other. But no matter where you go in this country, you'll never get away from being made to know that you are a Negro."

"Yes, sir," I said.

"We're aliens in an alien land." (And yet he had fought the Garveyites' dream of going "back to Africa"; had applauded the deportation of Emma Goldman; on every day of national memorial had hung out the flag, and when the breezes of May, the suns of July and the snows of February rent and seared it, had bought another!) "But there's some purpose in it," he went on wearily. "'God works in mysterious ways . . .' There's certainly some purpose. So do your best. Remember you're a Negro."

"I'll remember," I said, knowing that I would, because I had been well and exactly taught and because such lessons thrust deep. But feeling even then, I like to think, the iron unfairness of it; perhaps even drawing a sorry comfort from it, like many a Negro boy before and since. For after all, it is a ready-made excuse. More, it is license for us all to live in that blind, egoistic immaturity which, even under the most wholesome learning, we are reluctant to forego anyway. "Twice as much twice better. . . ."

"A Negro's just as good as anybody else," my father said, "but he's always got to prove it."

Thus burdened, I went off to college.

7

THE ASSUMPTIONS THAT WERE HELD valid in my boyhood were all wrong. So much has been said about them that I mention them reluctantly, but their strength is attested by the fact that many, many still trust them. And not merely Southern whites, and the misinformed, and the ignorant; nor whites alone, but blacks. Hodding Carter, novelist and Pulitzer prize-winning journalist, no doubt deserves his reputation as a Southern liberal, but only a few months ago he wrote of "a common insistence upon white political domination in the South," which is "as unbreakable as anything woven by the mind of man," and declared himself unalterably committed to race segregation on the ground of preserving the white race's "ethnic integrity." Somewhat earlier, the Georgia Commissioner of Agriculture had said, "The yellow people, the brown people and the blacks"— not even bothering to add "people"—"are mentally unfit for directors in our form of government." And in 1951 Kerr Scott, the Governor of North Carolina ("most liberal state in the South") echoed the Georgian. Asked by a Negro reporter why his inaugural promise had been fulfilled only to the extent of making one Negro appointment, the Governor snapped, "If I were you I'd never have asked that question. I have given you [people] more than you can handle.

. . . That's why I tell you you should never have asked that question."

So the old assumptions hold: the assumption of the Negro's inherent inferiority; of tragic social and cultural consequences if segregation is broken down on any but the most superficial levels; of Negroes preferring segregation, and many more. They were taken on in the first place as rationalizations by means of which the white man tried, as Gunnar Myrdal says, "to build a bridge of reason" between his acclaimed equalitarian creed and his countervailing deed. Because of this guilt-ridden adoption, they were the more avidly loved. They were also the more furiously drummed into the general consciousness where, reverberating like thunder in a valley, they have rolled out the tune to which white people and Negroes have danced since 1900—the Negroes because they must.

It is a static but a curiously hectic dance. We gyrate through its complicated patterns with responses as conditioned and involuntary as reflexes. In spite of all the fervent clapping and shouting, our reactions to the race problem are not really emotional and intellectual, but muscular. I cannot now, as long ago I could, believe in the moral and intellectual conviction of the demagogues, of men like Richard Russell and James Byrnes and Strom Thurmond; for I cannot believe that the findings of modern science are so cabined and confined, even in South Carolina, Georgia and Mississippi, as to have escaped the knowledge of these educated men. The older demagogues had this to excuse them; they were ignorant. The younger ones are knowing puppeteers, cynically manipulating the strings of the past.

And even the masses who respond to the strings know better than they used to; even with them conviction flags and cynicism takes over. The moral conviction that it was for the social welfare that they reserved all power to themselves no longer operates.

Power for power's sake is now the rule, and when a leading Georgia politician said so in a political address, the rafters rang. "We have the power and we mean to keep it where it belongs. If the Negroes vote wholesale, and if the county unit system goes, we'll have that much less power. But it must not go. The county unit system, which used to protect our rural population from slick city politics, now arms us all with power against the enemies of white supremacy."

The old assumptions hold, but, worse, others have been added to evade the knowledge that cannot now be ignored and to make possible the conformity to the vicious dialectic of power which rings as plangently in America now as in the rest of the world. And the chief of them is this—that hostility is the accepted state in which to live. Dualism is looked on as the natural division of absolute opposites, of enemies: Communism and democracy, Eastern man and Western man, native and foreign, and, most pertinent to this argument, black and white. Not black as formerly —the pathetically weak and erring child of nature; nor white as formerly—the tolerant chastiser and protector, the strong adult. But black raised by the findings of science (and the decisions of the highest court in the land) to close equality with white, and therefore the enemy to white.

Exaggerated? But toward truth, not away from it. That competition, which was once confined to the lowest economic levels and which resulted in the legendary hatred of the poor-white masses for the Negro and vice versa, operates on higher levels now. It is on the level of skilled labor, as the Brotherhood of Locomotive Engineers and Firemen knew when they brought suit to enjoin railroads from promoting Negro firemen (also members of the Brotherhood) to engineers. It is on the level of education, and persons reported to be students of the medical college of the University of South Carolina admitted sending threatening letters to a Negro applicant and burning a cross on his front lawn. It is on the level of the professions, so that a committee of the National Bar Association, a Negro group, felt constrained to report that "as the quality of training rises, Negro lawyers find it harder to win admission to the bar in some Southern states."

Actually, of course, it is no longer possible to predicate discrimination and segregation on Negro inferiority. So long as it was possible and seemed forever possible, the "practical-minded" found a kind of social justification in disfranchisement, in raising economic and cultural barriers, in the despotic paternalism which said, "Thou shalt not." Even *the* Negro leader, Booker Washington, found it blameless and, indeed, good, without ever suspecting that the tradition of *noblesse oblige,* on which all this was claimed to be founded, might someday be as ineffective as necromancy. Segregation was order; it was control; it was the steel and concrete casing sealing up a devastating social explosion. It still seems so to the vast majority and their leaders.

The strongest voices in the South today say that segregation must be kept: Governor James Byrnes in his inaugural was not so intent on expressing his views on foreign policy that he did not assure his listeners of his unaltered opposition to the Fair Deal. Hodding Carter, the liberal mentioned above, is not so liberal that he does not see it as "tragic for the South, the Negro, and the nation itself" if segregation is done away with. And "only a fool," Lillian Smith quotes from the Atlanta *Constitution,* "would say the Southern pattern of separation of the races can, or should be overthrown." But if segregation must be kept, it must now be predicated on something else than Negro inferiority.

And what else is there? The cynical ideology of power-worship, what H. A. Overstreet calls "the fight-and-grab image," the philosophy of hate. It is what Hitler came to. It is the result of a pattern of thinking desperately threatened by science and social change.

8

I AM AN INTEGRATIONIST. I HAVE BEEN
for a long time. It is not a principle that I arrived at
through intellection. Until the past few years, I did
not bring to bear on it whatever intelligence I have.
I felt my way to it, just as some men, in spite of ob-
structing experience, feel their way to ideals of hon-
esty, sobriety and continence. Nor was the feeling of
my way wholly conscious. It was rather like the action of one who kicks and splashes frantically to save
himself from drowning and suddenly finds that he
has reached a shelf on which he can stand in the
river bed. His objective was not the shelf, but just to
be saved. I kicked and splashed in all directions, and
suddenly there I was.

I was an integrationist when the Communists camp-
ed almost nightly on my trail in the early 1930's and
lighted beckoning bright fires in the frightening dark
of that time. I did not believe then (any more than
now) that the moment the bars of segregation are
lifted all the white women of the South will fall into
the arms of Negro mates. Many of my acquaintances
gleefully professed to believe this and would just as
gleefully declare that Negroes lynched for rape had
been only unlucky in being caught with their always-
willing white paramours. They found substance for
this opinion in both fact and fiction, which too

loudly proclaimed the revulsive feeling of the white female for the Negro and the inviolable purity of white womanhood. My acquaintances believed that Southern whites protested too much.

And so, it seems, did the Communists. Or perhaps they did not. It could have been just a line and the carrying out of explicit directives on "How to Recruit Negroes in the Eastern States." It could have been that they played expertly on what they thought were the secret dreams of a young, green, mixed-up and lonely man.

I suppose all people suffer from these maladies, and especially from youth, in early adulthood; but I had more besides. I had a severe case of "Negrophophilia" which alternately wrenched my heart with hate and love. I was confused about the direction of my life and extremely doubtful (as I sometimes am today) of life's purpose. Whether naturally or through learning, I shrank from all but a handful of people, and some of these were a disappointment to me, and I have no doubt that I was a sore trial to them. I lacked social accommodation. I have never thought tolerance admirable as a principle either of adjustment or feeling, and I rejected it entirely for my friends. Dogs were to be tolerated, and crying babies, and strangers with whom one did not have to become acquainted. My friends were constantly not living up to my foolish expectations; my judgments were severe. I was continually breaking with and rejoining them, but with no increase in understanding.

I do not think I would have become a Communist even had these deficiencies not been in me. But, certainly, except for them, the Communists would have had an easier time assailing my weak position on the extreme left flank of democracy. The wrong scouts came to reconnoiter, and they took the wrong approach.

The first who came was a moist, sleazy fellow, fat

and asthmatic. I had often seen him in the little restaurant where I took dinner. Frequently he would be there in low-voiced conversation with various people—men and women—when I entered. He always sat at the round, family table back in the corner at an angle from the door, and my glance would fall there first. There would be beer before him (it was just legal again) and a dish of olives and olive pits and a plate of fried potatoes which he ate with his fingers. Though I did not think he was aware of me, no one could be unaware of him. Even from my table by the window and with my back squarely toward him, I was conscious of his presence. In lulls of dish rattling and conversation, his wheeze could be heard all over the tiny restaurant.

One evening when I went there later than usual, because I had waited for a cold rain to stop, and took my place, Eric, the German waiter, told me that "Philip" wanted to talk to me. He indicated the fat man at the big table. There was little possibility of Eric's having made a mistake. The restaurant had only a dozen tables and it catered to a limited and steady patronage of unimportant executives, clerks and apprentices from the jewelry manufactures and a few plebeian graduate students like myself. I do not remember ever seeing another Negro there. Even though Eric had made no mistake, I was sure that I did not want to talk to "Philip." But before I could put my thoughts into words and summon the courage to utter them, Philip was standing there. He looked at me expressionlessly as he pulled the chair far out —to allow for his pendulous belly—and sat down.

"This rain. My friends are all late tonight," he said. "You'll excuse me." There was nothing questioning, or tentative, or apologetic in the way he spoke. I was acutely embarrassed. He took a piece of potato out of the dish he had brought with him and carried it to his mouth. It was a small, full-lipped mouth. His hands, too, I noticed, were small and very white, though the nails and the knuckles were dirty, in contrast to his moist, flushed face.

"What does the 'J' in your name represent?" he asked. I was taken by surprise and must have shown it, for he blew out an indulgent laugh. "You wouldn't think I would know your name." This was not a question either. "I do." And he spoke it.

The sound of it coming from a complete stranger seemed to establish some kind of power over me. I felt a twinge of fright even, as if I were suddenly vulnerable in ways I knew not of.

"How do you know?"

He swung his head from side to side and his face smiled at me. "I know. And I know more," he said. He called off items of biographical fact as if he were reading from a file card—the year and place of my birth, my father's name, my brother's name, my schooling, an attack of scarlet fever I had had. Momentarily I half expected him to go into an account of monstrous crimes I had committed in some other and unremembered character. It seems silly now, for I know that to get such information as he had was an easy matter, but then I felt that for some dark purpose I could not guess a million pairs of eyes had followed me since birth.

I do not wish to play up this episode nor to dramatize my reaction to it, for what followed was ridiculous emotional anticlimax. Through the next talk Philip had with me a week or so later, his efforts to get on terms of easy familiarity dissipated my sense of being mysteriously overpowered and exposed. I did not respond to the first-name camaraderie. Not knowing his last name, I avoided calling him anything. I think my formal civility frustrated him, and I think this is why, in a kind of desperation during the third or fourth meeting, he pulled out a folder of very detailed obscene photographs and handed them

to me. He laughed when he asked in pretended casualness (for I could feel him watching me sharply) whether I had seen anything like them before. And weren't they the most amusing things, and one in particular, because he knew the girl in it—a student at the art school. He had some "delicious" friends, he said, and he would like me to meet them. He said that there was one "bonnie brunette especially, from 'way down in Georgia—but completely, and I mean completely, emancipated" and without prejudice. They lined up fast enough once they were really free, he said, and it only went to show what would happen to the race problem all over the country were it not for the strength and pressure of reaction. "There just wouldn't be any if it were left to the women."

I think Philip was running 'way ahead of his time-table. Or, to change the figure, he had cast his net on the wrong tide. There was not enough weight to it in any case. I knew later that there was quite a potential catch of assorted fish, including a young college student who wore very thick glasses, a French-descended politician who had considerable power in local labor circles, and a very wealthy widow in her late thirties. Even then the widow was contributing generously to the cell, and some years later she became nationally known as pro-Communist. There were others too, but I do not know how they had been approached, nor how many were caught. Perhaps Philip and those who joined him in subsequent weeks fumbled the assignment badly. At least this one got away. The approach to my intellect is not through my gonads.

One approach perhaps is through my curiosity, and it was curiosity that teased me into going here and there with Philip. I wanted to see what kind of people these were. I had listened to soapbox Communists on the streets of New York, but they had

aroused nothing in me save vague speculations over such questions as were bruited about in those days. What was wrong with our government? Did the rich and powerful think only to gain more power and reap more benefits from the exploitation of the working class? What should the government do? What could it do? What was Hoover doing that he should not do, and vice versa? I felt a certain shallow contempt for the emotionalism, the unreasoning bitterness and the actless anger of the soapbox radicals.

I do not know whether it was because they were a cohesive motley of white Americans, Negroes, Italians, Portuguese and French, but I liked better the brazen self-interest of the radical workers whom I had seen milling about the shut-down (what an ominous word that was!) blank-walled factories in southwest Providence. But I could not identify myself with them either. They talked of violence and did violence (as once when the police tried to scatter them) in an implacable, matter-of-fact way that repelled me. I have never believed in violence. I have heard Negroes advocate it. I once knew of a group of Negroes who organized to kill a white man every time a Negro was lynched. They called themselves the Kwick Kure Klub, Inc., in grim parody of the Ku Klux Klan. They were to have branches in every principal city of the South. Though it was rumored, and is still widely believed among Negroes, that the violent and unsolved murder of a constable in Greene County, Missouri, in the 1930's was the work of the black KKK, I think the organization never really got started.

Nor could I identify myself in more than a superficial way with the campus group of intellectual radicals with whom a common interest in writing brought me into contact. They were enthusiastic and well-meaning, but quite innocent and harmless. They knew considerably more about John Reed, Hey-

wood Broun and H. L. Mencken than about Marx, Lenin and the deviationism of Trotsky. They knew something about Nietzsche too, and they were learning, goggle-eyed, something about Freud. But the German philosopher's "will to power" was not translated into political terms, and Freud's *Civilization and Its Discontents*, which had only recently appeared in this country, was simply a yardstick by which they measured their imaginary personal gripes against smugness and conservatism. Theirs was the rebellion of youth. They talked a lot, but what they said was mostly brilliant nonsense which had no more relation to the actual destruction of the bridges over which their parents had passed than a pyrotechnic display on a moonless night. Only one of them became a writer—a humorist, and a good one. His latest book now lies before me. Sensitive, talented, some of them wealthy, they turned out to be thoroughly conservative college professors, investment brokers and lawyers who had no trouble making a peace with things as they are.

My problems were different from theirs. The drives —self-preservation, anxiety, vanity, sex, the "Complete discharge of strength" Nietzsche speaks of— were considerably modified by my Negroness. Such an admission is embarrassing to make, but I recognized its truth even then. Self-preservation, for instance, was not a galvanic drive in me, nor in other Negroes I knew. I have written elsewhere that five of my closest acquaintances committed suicide in a span of six red and terrible years. Pride and vanity were excessive. Since Negroes were assumed to be sexually immoderate, I made a show of strict asceticism, chastising the flesh in a way most unnatural to youth. What I did not recognize was that I was being forced into the narrowest egocentrism; into an involvement with self that was morbid beyond reason and that only the lucky are able to sublimate—

and this only partially—into group concern and, with extreme luck, wider social concern. It need not be said, and certainly not in the way of apology, that this is not altogether the fault of the Negro. It is the fault also of the American life-situation—neither quite an accidental wickedness ror a complex of impersonal coercions—over which both the individual and the group control of minority people is limited.

The campus group of intellectual radicals broadened me. They stimulated my reading, my imagination, my sympathies. To the reading of James, Santayana and DeUnamuno, to whom Professor Ducasse had introduced me, I added Nietzsche (especially *Thus Spake Zarathustra*) and Marx and much else that I would not have come across in the ordinary routine of my graduate study.

But I was not broadened enough to take what Philip and his circle offered. Had their offerings stayed on the level of the first parties I attended with Philip, matters might have been different. I can take any amount of talk, and there ran through their rapid-fire conversations phrases that, exploding like firecrackers, drew my attention: "the political state" (as distinct from the economic and social state—they were drawing such distinctions then); "the omnicompetent state"; "responsibility in areas of cultural autonomy." Of course I had ideas as to meanings, but nothing they said really coalesced into concepts. I was not moved either to agreement or disagreement. I simply heard.

In later meetings, however, I began to listen and to understand, but not what it was expected I would understand. Rather the opposite. I began to comprehend that they talked like people who had a vested interest in a democratic catastrophe. It was not Communism's strength and validity, its constructive and health-seeking activities on which they based their arguments: it was democracy's weaknesses. They rejoiced in the economic depression because they saw in it the beginning of democracy's total collapse. The idea, they said, was security *and* freedom (and I agreed with this), but under "your system"—they were talking directly to me and to Hakely, a young but grizzled silversmith apprentice—"there is neither." They were too smart actually to make capitalism and democracy synonymous, so I could judge only that this equating one with the other was a deliberate effort to confuse.

And I was confused, and I showed it in childish exasperation at the way in which they pointed out, with a kind of glib, cold fervor, every weakness, every failure, every instance of corruption and discrimination and injustice, and how these affected one personally, and especially the Negro. The inference was plain that in the "omnicompetent state," the "service state" (which were equated), these things would not be. But when I pressed for proof of their inferences, Philip and the intellectual leaders of the cell withdrew into taunts and challenges and were not percipient enough to see how dangerously they threatened my self-esteem. The idea of democracy was itself not particularly dear to me then, but I resented the doubts cast on my inherited assumptions about it. If anything, I resented democracy for leaving me and itself so defenseless; but I hated Communism for putting me on the defensive. My anger and frustration carried over from one meeting to the next, for though their arguments were basically weak, I had no answers to them. After the fifth meeting, I was certain that I was through with the Communists and all their works.

But I did not figure on the proselyting passion of Philip and Honey. This latter was one of the five women in the cell whom I had seen regularly at meetings. "Honey" was a cell nickname, and it suited only her physical appearance. Among her colleagues

at the city hospital, where she told me she worked as
a technician, she was known as Branca. I never
learned her last name. Of foreign extraction—Aus-
trian or Czech, I judged—she had soft honey-blond
hair, worn in a long bob, so that when she turned or
lowered her head a wave of hair fell across her face.
It was a good face, not pretty and decorated, but
well-structured and strong, with pale yellow eyes set
under square brows. She talked a great deal in a rather
strident and insolent tone, and she laughed a lot, in-
solently too. Both her laughter and her talk seemed
to come from very near the surface. Yet one felt that
she had depths. Sometimes one was as hard put to
follow the erratic train of her thought as to follow
her restless, vital movements.

Philip and Honey came to my lodginghouse one
night after I had twice failed to show up at meetings. It was embarrassing to have them come there,
for my landlady, though she had been born and had
lived all her life in New England and though she
thought that this was in itself some sort of victory or
credit for a Negro—my landlady was only less suspicious of white people than she was of Negroes
who consorted with them. Even had they desired it,
my visitors could not have come in, so I went with
them to the two untidy rooms which Honey occupied
over a delicatessen in the oldest and a-step-from-
genteel section of the city. There were just the three
of us, and over a bottle of very sour wine, which
was called dago red, they questioned me about my
absences. I told them that I had been preparing for
midyear examinations, which was true, and anyway
was I to consider myself obligated to be present at
every cell meeting?

They looked at each other for a moment. Then
Honey laughed deliciously and said, "Of course not,"
and Philip laboriously wheezed an echo of this. In
cell meetings Philip was the center, but here Honey

had complete charge. She led the talk into all sorts of
trivial channels. Shifting restlessly in her chair, tossing
her head, crossing and uncrossing her legs, Honey
talked and talked. Her vitality and the wine were
exhilarating. She was profane and final in her judgments of people. She jokingly accused Philip of trying to bring into the cell some "profound asses,"
some "absolutely untouchable unteachables," like a
certain Sidney she mentioned, who was positively,
she said, a "reconditioned pervert." Oh, she was sure
of it! And Faye Hariston (this was the wealthy
widow), who "every day jumped into a barrel of
peroxide," and who, for all her efforts at femininity,
showed that she was a "conditioned hermaphrodite."
Laughing gaily, Honey wanted to know what Philip
was doing, recruiting people for his own pleasure?
Was that what he was making of the cell, a circle
of Lesbians and libertines?

Unembarrassed and unsmiling, Philip only shook
his head, and after a time Honey went on to something else. The atmosphere was very casual, very
friendly, and I was sorry when Philip announced that
he must leave. It was my cue to go too, and I got
up.

There was a moment's hesitation before Philip said,
"Oh, but I'll be back! You wait for me here." I
looked at Honey, but she was already reclaiming the
hat I had picked up. I thought she smiled mockingly
at Philip.

What Honey and I talked about after Philip's de-
parture, I do not know. In my notebook the next day
I wrote exactly what follows.

"I wish I could make out a case of moral recti-
tude for myself, but I cannot. What I kept thinking
of last night was all the possible consequences. When
Honey came and sat on the couch too close to me, I
remembered all I had heard about 'parlor whores'—
that they were bold and brazen and without dis-

crimination, and that they were bound to be diseased. I had never had more than a dozen words with her until last night, so there was no affection for me. There was only passion, and even this may not have been genuine. I half wished it were, or that I could think it so. My feeling was that her object was to arouse passion in me while she kept herself out of it and under control. She shivered and rolled her head against my shoulder and dug her nails into my thigh, but I think that it was all faked. I do not not know what we talked about between times, or whether we talked about anything.

"But if she were outside it, I was outside it too, and I kept thinking that Honey had some ulterior motive and that she was trying to realize it at too high a price. I knew that she wanted me to have sex relations with her and I knew also that I would not, could not, dared not. I do not think she tempted me at all, really; she just frightened me. I did not see how anyone could go to such a length to obtain a result that in the long run could have almost no importance. Certainly I cannot think myself *that* important to the Communists. And suppose this were not her reason? Then what? Just sex. I cannot trust a white woman that way. No matter how willingly a white woman gives herself to a colored man, if she is found out, she will yell rape. Last night I pictured newspaper headlines such as I have seen many times and I thought of them referring to me: BLACK BRUTE. I did the right thing last night, though maybe I did it for all the wrong reasons."

I fled. Though I knew I had done the right thing, I was ashamed to see Honey and Philip again, for I convinced myself that I had been naïf and cowardly. I did not go back to the little restaurant at the bottom of the hill. Once I had a note from Philip, and once he—or someone very like him—inquired of me from my landlady, but I did not see him, nor

Honey, nor any of the people I used to see in the cell. I am certain that Honey, laughing with strident insolence, spoke of me as one of Philip's "untouchable unteachables," and pretty quickly forgot me.

9

_____

BUT I DID NOT FORGET COMMUNISM, then or later. In New York the next year, 1933, the Party was quite fashionable among my acquaintances, some of whom took it seriously. One could be sure that among the guests at Harlem's middle and upper-class social gatherings would be white people and that these were admitted Communists or fellow travelers at least. Some of them were said to be well known in *avant-garde* and esoteric circles and in the theater but I had never heard of most of them, and I am inclined to think that the reputations they were given in Harlem were a kind of defense in depth against the allegation that the only whites Negroes could mingle with socially were peripheral people, nobodies, tramps. The white people I met at such parties seemed average intellectual types. I was struck by the fact that they did not talk Communism, but gave the impression of living on a higher and freer level than American democracy afforded. The atmosphere they created was easy and sophisticated, with a high sexual content of which, it was said, nearly everyone took advantage. No one bothered to whisper the stories of liaisons between white women and Negro men and Negro women and white men. They were accepted without shock, and the actors in these little dramas seemed to play their roles with a lack of embarrassment and even a natural grace that fascinated me.

I do not think any of the Communists I met in these circumstances were seriously political-minded. Certainly they were not Party workers. They did not make speeches from flag-draped stepladders wedged against curbings, as so many Communists were doing daily in front of the Home Relief stations scattered over the city. They did not rustle up meetings, nor belong to instructional cells, nor try to indoctrinate anyone. They were not of the "soiled shirt, sinkers and coffee brigade." My Negro acquaintances would not have had them in their homes if they had been. Communism was merely the rose under which they pursued more pleasurable activities.

There were a good many hastily printed Communist leaflets being passed out in those days. I seemed to get them all; I also read them. They were slanted for the middle-class Negro—the professional, the intellectual, the student. With only half an eye one could see that the Party was conducting a campaign to recruit a potential, educated Negro leadership. The labor masses had been a disappointment to the Communists who, anyway, employed the wrong methods to enlist them. Negro labor was far from ready for the proletarian revolution. It was not class struggle but race struggle that interested them. What the Negro labor masses wanted was to be treated as a special case first. They wanted job security. They wanted to be brought up to the level of white workers before they could march in the ranks with them toward the bigger Communist goal. Equality first, and then integration. Besides, Negro labor had the same suspicion of Communism that it had of socialism and trade-unionism—a suspicion of being used rather than helped, and used for the establishment of an order of things that was not quite clear.

So the new recruitment was to be among the class

of which I was an inconsequential representative. The Communists were determined not to make the same mistake twice. *Equality, Land and Freedom: A Program for Negro Liberation,* issed by the League of Struggle for Negro Rights in 1933, put it this way: "The task that confronts the . . . Party in organizing the Negro workers and rallying them for the daily class struggle . . . side by side with the white workers is no light one. . . . The Negro evinces no militant opposition towards Communism, but he wants to know how it can improve his social status, what bearing does it have on the common practice of lynching, political disfranchisement, segregation, industrial discrimination. . . . The Negro is revolutionary enough in a racial sense. . . ." In short, he is race-conscious, and this was enough to concentrate on. In the late 1920's and the early 1930's, the Communists got some good advice from somewhere. They also took advantage of two circumstances.

The Angelo Herndon case was still bubbling and boiling and the Scottsboro case was just reaching another of its vociferous climaxes in 1933. The International Labor Defense was formed in those days, and I met William L. Patterson, its secretary. Next to James D. Ford, the Communist Party's Vice-Presidential nominee in 1932, Patterson held the highest rank of any Negro in the Party. But I was not impressed by him. He seemed of small intellectual caliber, though very ambitious and bold. I was more impressed by a well-known and engaging Negro journalist. He had just returned from Russia (and, I suppose, a period of indoctrination) when I met him backstage at the Fourteenth Street Theatre, where *Stevedore* was playing. I can remember his saying to me, "We Negro writers have a great opportunity and an inflexible duty to promote the revolution that will extirpate caste, class and race." How flattering! "We Negro writers—" to lump me in with Langston Hughes,

Claude McKay, Jean Toomer, Rudolph Fisher, Countee Cullen and himself, all of them talented, all of them well known. He could not possibly have heard of me—I had written and published professionally only one story at that time. But the Negro art and literary "renaissance" had not waned enough for those close to it to see that it was fading, and now and then, a completely unknown student, I basked in that artificial light like a homeless beggar keeping himself warm over a sidewalk grating.

But Communism gave off a light of a different quality. It had no comfort in it. As harsh and as revealing as the light in a surgical operating room, it cast no cozy shadow into which one could slip for those moments of quiet reflection which seemed as necessary to me as food and drink. Communism did not allow for the play of individual thought and initiative. It had no warmth in it. Or perhaps it is untrue to say this, since intense heat and intense cold produce the same primary reaction—a shriveling up, a drying out, until the living thing loses its own identity and becomes one with the heat or the cold. I saw something of this reaction in New York and I was appalled by it. Or perhaps this too is untrue. Perhaps what appalled me was the realization that there were people who felt themselves so helplessly cast out of American society and democratic reckoning that they could suck with voracious hunger at the cold breast of Communism. One of the things I could not understand was the unquestioning submission to control.

I do not mean to give the impression that I met many avowed Negro Communists. I did not—not more than a half dozen in all. But with one of them I had nearly seven months of close association. He had a room next to mine in the place where I was living and we shared a bath. He was a thief. He did not make his living in this way. He had to do with the stock and delivery room of a garmentmaking firm, he told me, and he was a minor official in a local union of either truckers or garmentmakers, I do not know which. He was a thief solely for the benefit of the Party. That was his Party work and his duty and he served it blindly. It was a strange work. At more or less regular intervals he stole bolts of cloth—"suitings" was his word—and kept them in his room until someone, seldom the same person twice, identifying himself by some prearranged means, made contact and relieved him of the goods. He never knew what happened to them ultimately.

Curiously enough this was almost the only information about himself Clark (we will call him) ever volunteered, and of course I did not know this at first. What I did know about Clark—but only after probing —was that he came originally from Pennsylvania and had been graduated from a high school in one of the towns in that state. When the CCC agency was organized, he applied for admission to one of the work groups, but was rejected because high school was supposed to have given him a vocation by means of which he could earn a living. Caught in the depression, without money and, I gathered, without stable family connections, he drifted for a while—to Pittsburgh, to Philadelphia and finally to New York. He was a rugged-looking, stiff-faced young man of twenty-four or twenty-five. One would never suspect from his appearance or from his unimpassioned manner of speaking what a steady flame of fanaticism burned in him. He did not talk well. His voice was coarse, his tongue slightly thick, and he had a very limited command of the language. He spoke of this one day after we had got to know each other fairly well.

"I wish I could talk—like you," he said. I was about to protest that I was no model, when he added, "Or like James Ford." This was a complete letdown for me. I had both seen and heard James Ford when he was stumping the Eastern seaboard for the League of Struggle for Negro Rights, and I did not think much of him. He seemed basically ignorant, like a parrot fluently repeating phrases he had been carefully taught. His manner seemed gross.

"James Ford?"

"If I could talk like him, maybe I could be where he is now," Clark said.

"And where is he?" I genuinely wanted to know. I had heard nothing of him since his farcical campaign as the Communist Party's Vice-Presidential candidate.

"I don't know, but I think he's in Russia," Clark said.

"You want to go to Russia? But why?"

"What's this country ever done for me? What am I here?" he asked impassively. "A nigger anybody can spit on. In Russia I could be a man." This too came without anger or bitterness, and I could understand it. He was giving idiomatic expression to a simple wish for dignity and self-respect. One heard it so often among Negroes that one was likely to forget the deep wound of denial which it covered like a scab.

"I know a fellow who went to Russia," I said brightly. "Apparently he likes it. He's never come back."

"He's got the right idea. I wouldn't come back neither, if I ever went."

"It doesn't appeal to me," I said. "You've been listening to the guys on the stepladder, the Reds, across the street."

Clark gave me then a long, slow look, but there was nothing in it that I could detect—no quickening either of speculation or resentment. "I'm a Communist," he said.

I laughed with surprise and embarrassment and, still with his passive eyes on me, he said again, "I'm a Communist," bluntly.

There was nothing to say and so I kept silent, and to keep silent with Clark was like nothing so much as expecting to be talked to by a wall. He went to his own room shortly. The next day when we met, I felt a little twinge of embarrassment, but he seemed not to, and the feeling soon passed.

Though I did not know it then, I talked to Clark for next to the last time less than a month later. He came to my room one night, as he often did, but this time he announced phlegmatically that he was in trouble. He neither looked nor sounded like a man in trouble and I could think only that he was in trouble with a girl—though girls had never been a subject of conversation between us.

"What kind of trouble?" I inquired.

I suppose Clark lacked a certain sensitiveness, though I would not have called him callous. I do not think it was because he did not care: it was just that he could not estimate the effect his words had upon others.

"I'm a thief and I think they suspicion me," he said.

I must have said something like "Oh, go on," or "Quit kidding," but I knew he had no sense of humor and was quite incapable of kidding. I looked at him. He seemed to think I had not heard him. "I'm a thief and I think they suspicion me," he repeated. And when he took me to his room and showed me a flat-top trunk half full of bolts of cloth, I believed him.

"But what are you going to do with this stuff? If they suspect you and come——"

"I'm going to get shut of it," he said stoically. "I'm going to get shut of it now in a few minutes." He was stuffing the bolts of cloth into two battered valises.

"What are you going to do? How are you going to get rid of it?"

This time he did not answer, but swung the valises off the bed, brushed past me and went down the hall.

The next time (and the last time) I talked with Clark was in the Ninth Precinct jail. He was arrested on a Saturday. On Sunday a newspaper reporter who covered the precinct telephoned me, saying that Clark wanted to see me. I did not like it. I was vexed by the fear of somehow becoming involved in his trouble. I went with reluctance. The desk sergeant, I thought, eyed me suspiciously when I asked for Clark but perhaps it was just my nervousness, for he called another officer who, taking a key, led me through some doors and along a tier of empty cells. Clark was in the last cell on the tier and he must have heard us coming, for I found him standing expectantly. He smiled stiffly when he saw me, but waited until the policeman had gone before he spoke.

"They got me," he said.

My mood was not pleasant, I'm afraid, nor talkative. I had no wish to draw him out. If he had anything to say to me, I thought, then he would damned well say it without help from me. He was still smiling stiffly.

"They got me," he said again.

"So I see," I said. "Now what?"

They were holding him for a preliminary hearing on Monday, he said. Then, as if it were something which did not concern him—as if he were speaking of someone else who was altogether a stranger to him— he told me of his work for the Communists as I have related it above. I could not understand it. I stared at him, for what he was saying sounded crazy, especially to be coming in so calm and uninflected a voice.

"But why?" I wanted to know.

"It was my job," he said, as if that explained it truly and entirely; as if it completely satisfied the demands of my question.

"What did you send for me for? I can't do anything

55

for you," I said. "Somebody's made a fool of you. Let them look out for you."

"You got it all wrong," he said, shaking his head slowly.

"You've got it all wrong. You're in jail," I said bitingly.

"But I ain't no fool, unless doing things for a good point is one. And I don't want nobody to look out for me."

"Well, if you did, somebody else would have to do it."

"What could they do? You want me to get them in trouble?"

"You mean the Communists?"

"My action group," he said. "They can't do nothing. They ain't supposed to do nothing."

I stared at him with even greater intensity. "They know and they won't even go bail for you or get you a lawyer?" My outraged credulity was as lost on him as my vexation had been.

"I told you," he said.

"You mean it's supposed to be this way? You knew that if something like this happened, your action group wouldn't do anything?"

"I ain't going to drag nobody else in," he said doggedly.

"They shouldn't have to be dragged in," I said, and I think I raised my voice in exasperation. "They ought to come in."

"You wrong," he said.

"But you're the one who's in jail."

I could not believe that what was happening to him could happen. Of course I had heard stories of strict Party discipline, of orders being given to Party members to do what no one in his right mind would do, but I had not believed such stories, though they were common and though they were also congruous with the newspaper accounts of the purges that were then taking place in Russia. I had kept my reservations. But this business with Clark was real. He was someone I knew, and this was happening to him.

"Look," I said, "why don't you be sensible? Why don't you——"

He was shaking his head before I could finish. There seemed to be nothing I could say to arouse him to a true recognition of the fix he was in. Perhaps at bottom he had a martyr complex, but I could not see in him any of the things I associated with martyrdom. There was none of the fire, none of the dignity and nobility I thought of as belonging in the picture. There were not even defiance and rebellion in him— or if they were, Clark kept them hidden beneath layers of stony reserve that could not be penetrated. Besides, it seemed to me that to *have* to suffer alone for a principle made the principle suspect.

And he suffered alone. I did not go to see him in the Tombs where he was remanded after the preliminary hearing, and on the day of his trial I searched four papers before I found in one of them a short notice: NEGRO CONVICTED OF THEFT.

I saw him again at the trial. It lasted less than twenty minutes. Clark, in the same rumpled brown suit he had worn in jail, was led in. He looked slightly drawn, but I think I was the only one of the twenty or thirty spectators who could have known this. No one seemed to take any interest in this fourth case on the docket. The charge was read. The court-appointed lawyer pleaded guilty. A short, stocky man was sworn in and gave testimony to the effect that so-many and so-many bolts of cloth were missing over a period of months; that company detectives were put on the trail of them, and that finally in March they had found "their man." Then a private detective testified; then a stock clerk. There were no other witnesses.

Clark was ordered to stand. The judge pronounced sentence—five years in prison. Clark looked around at the spectators then, but I could see no change in his expression. He was nudged away. I left the courtroom.

10

LIKE THE CAPACITY FOR THOUGHT AND the desire for knowledge, the instincts for personal liberty and, within reason, power over one's destiny are attributes of the human mind. They are stronger in some than in others. Where they have been weakened by catastrophe—say long-continued planned violence, as in war; or widespread social disorganization, as in times of great economic crises—the instincts can be perverted, or even totally destroyed. There was danger of this perversion (which actually developed in some countries in Europe) during America's great depression, when the feeling grew that only Franklin D. Roosevelt had answers and that everything depended on him. The American people were all but ripe to surrender their minds and the control of their destiny.

It was the distortion or atrophy of this instinct that the Communists hoped to find in the American Negro. They had good reason for such hopes, and they were not loath to express it: "The especially intense exploitation and heavy oppression to which the millions of Negroes in America are subject make it imperative for *the Party to devote its best energies and its maximum resources towards becoming the recognized leader and champion . . . of Negroes.** (Italics

* Jay Lovestone, "The Sixth World Congress of the Communist International," *Communist*, VII, No. 11; Nov. 1928, pp. 673-674.

mine.) The intense exploitation and heavy oppression
were true enough. But there was something that the
Communists did not take into account; something
psychical and perhaps unworldly which even the
people whom they hoped to inveigle did not think
about. It was not the Negro's vaunted resiliency,
though this was something. Rather it was what I can
think of only as the spiritual cohesion of democracy.
This cohesion is organic to the delicately balanced
ideological structure that democracy is, and it is the
attribute which makes it impossible to separate
the destiny of America from the destiny of democracy
itself.

For democracy is less a form of government than
it is a way of life, and the principles—freedom, equality, justice—on which this way of life is founded have
an appeal as universal as the idea of God. And what
I am saying is that in spite of "heavy oppression" and
"intense exploitation," the American Negro believed
in the principles. It was this belief in the principles
and the impossibility of ever dissociating them
in the Negro's mind from democracy and America that
stymied the Communists, who could not understand
why the colored people's hatred of discrimination,
segregation and all the inequities did not lead naturally to a hatred of democracy. But it was like expecting them to hate God because preachers are sometimes rascals.

Nor do I think that this is as abstruse and metaphysical as it sounds. Or if it is, then it is well to remember that American democracy is itself a metaphysic,
blending as it does subjective truth ("the inalienable
rights of man") with moral abstractions ("liberty and
justice for all") and mystical concepts ("the will of
the people") which admittedly cannot be achieved
by all the institutions ever created by man. It is,
this democracy, "impractical." It was this that the
Communists took cognizance of and figured on. They

did it three times between 1918 and 1942, and each time in crisis, when they thought the material values which they wished to substitute as the goal of struggle were enhanced by their very absence. The terms they used were purely materialistic too, and they applied them in a context that was unbounded by the American continent—and this was another mistake. "The American Communist Negroes," the Communists said, "are the historical leaders of their comrades in Africa and to fit them for dealing the most telling blows to world imperialism as allies of the world's working class is enough to justify all the time and energy that the Workers (Communist) Party must devote to the mobilization for the revolutionary struggle of the Negro workers in American industry." *

Then they tried to extirpate the spiritual values of democracy by extirpating Christianity. They did not carry on a full-scale campaign of godlessness among American Negroes, but the Negro poet Langston Hughes, who went to visit Russia as a Guest of the State, came back apparently spiritually callous and published the poem "Goodbye, Christ," and the appalling fact was lost on no one. By and large, Negroes did not feel that Christ and religion were ready for the discard, certainly not before they had been tried. Indeed, their egalitarian aspirations had their roots in Biblical injunction. So the purge of the priests, the smashing of ikons, and the tearing down of the churches, which Negroes read about in the American press, were factors in the failure of the Communist Party to win the support of the black masses.

Add to this one other matter, and the whole story (though oversimplified) of that failure is told. Add patriotism. In some sophisticated Negro circles it

* William F. Dunne, "Negroes in American Industries," *Workers Monthly*, IV, No. 6; Apr. 1925.

is a matter for amused laughter that no Negro has ever been a traitor to the United States. But the laughter does not abrogate the fact. More perhaps than other American minorities, Negroes have had inducements to treachery. Clark expressed it: "What has this country ever done for me?" And of course Negroes before and since have asked the same question. It is purely rhetorical. Clark did not realize it, but America, its ideals, its direction, its basic spirit (for we must again deal with abstractions) had given him a belief in the individual worth and dignity of himself as a man. DuBois, I think, was right when, back in his young, good days, he said, "First, this is our country: we have worked for it, we have suffered for it, we have fought for it . . . we have reached in this land our highest modern development and nothing, humanly speaking, can prevent us from eventually reaching here the full stature of our manhood. . . . Our wrongs are still wrong [but] we will not bargain with our loyalty."

I am just cynical enough to add a sour note. This loyalty comes in part from a fear of expulsion. It is a historic fear, stemming back to the colonization movement in the seventeenth century. Recently Negroes have seen another minority in other countries expelled, and they know it can be done. But American Negroes have no Palestine.

I will not say that Negroes saw democracy as the highest, final product of man's political development nor that they saw enough differences between Communism and democracy to reassure them of the worth of the latter. They did not come to that stage of intellection—and neither did I until much later. I do not think that even the Negro Communists, so recently in the news, with all their reputation for mental acumen, have thought much about the real differences. For actually, of course, the Communist doctrine, like the dogma of the most fundamental religious sect, does not encourage thought. If it did, there probably would be less than a villageful of Communists in the whole Western world, for it would be seen that Communism is a falling away from the idea that the Western world has lived by since the Middle Ages—the idea that *man* is the end of all human endeavor, and that mere "survival and security" are not enough for man. But this distinction is only gross enough to explain why Communism is the ideology of crisis; why it must seize its chance to win men's minds when their highest hope is only to stave off death. No, even the intellectuals seem not to have seen this; and the other distinctions are subtler, finer. But they are also fundamental.

First of all, Communism is revolution, a rupture of order, a break in the evolution of Western civilization. Democracy, on the other hand, is a way of conducting affairs so that there is some kind of harmonious continuity in the direction of society. There may be errors and blunders, and there are certainly lags, but the people in a democracy are themselves so sensitive that they automatically exert a corrective force in the way a ship's gyroscope does. This sensitiveness is the strength of democracy. Communism must operate within a relatively simple but rigid structure (like the "classless society") with a narrow philosophic base and narrowly defined aims, so that the prestige of authority can be enhanced to tyrannical proportions and so that the decrees of authority can be immediately and continuously checked. There is no margin either for error or disagreement. Democracy is a complex way of life, lacking the utter concentration of energy in any one direction (save in time of national emergency) that marks Communism and that makes no allowance for opposing points of view. Communism must drastically curtail man's freedom in the first place, prescribe his rights and privileges in the second, and finally it must stand constantly ready to alienate those rights—by force, if necessary, or by the show of force, or by the implication of force. Democracy seeks a constant enlargement of man's freedom. Because in modern times Communism has seemed able to establish itself only by violence, it seems reasonable to assume that violence is necessary to its perpetuation, while at the same time it is more susceptible to disintegration through violence. Under Communism, man is the slave of the state. Under democracy, the state is the servant of man.

If all this editorializing sounds somewhat beside the point, since only peripherally does it have to do with my Negroness, then I can only plead that it seems to me a description of the sober facts, and that it is by way of being an explanation to the Communists of my anti-Communism. I should have given it to them ten years ago. They should have had it back in 1942 when, after a ten-year layoff, the Communists came at me again and made it necessary for me to try to achieve a certain degree of clarity about these issues.

I had written a book called *No Day of Triumph*, and the Communists saw advance copies of it. They liked it, though I am still puzzled why. Perhaps it was because I did not actually condemn Communism, but, as a matter of fact, expressed sympathy for one Mike Chowan who had long been a Communist and who had fought with the Lincoln Battalion in Spain. Whatever the reason, *New Masses* first published an excerpt from my book, without, as I remember, getting either my permission or that of the publisher. Soon after the *New Masses* excerpt appeared and several weeks before publication, I began to get letters from Communists all over the country. Some of these came from bookstore managers who told me that they were going to push the book and who invited me to teas and to hold autograph parties. I accepted only one of these invitations—to speak to a group in Washington, where I had to go on other business anyway. Later I was asked to appear on a radio program with Ella Winters in Philadelphia, but a previous commitment interfered.

A little while after publication, I went to New York to attend a dinner party for Carl Van Vechten. When that was over sometime after midnight, without quite realizing what we were in for, my wife and I accepted an invitation to another gathering, and found ourselves in an apartment on West 56th Street, surrounded by a motley crowd who told me that they were going to make *No Day of Triumph* a best seller. They were going to put me, as a writer, they said, in the same income class with Howard Fast and Richard Wright, who, they claimed, but for them, would not have been where they were. Toward dawn, what seemed to be a committee of three cornered me in the kitchenette and asked me whether I would sign a card. I said I would have to think about it. What I have written above is what I thought.

11

So far as i know, no one from the outside has ever tried to infect the Negro group with fascism. There have been some inside the group, but, excepting Marcus Garvey, I do not think they were consciously fascist. Negro colleges have tended to breed fascism—I would say a mild form of it, except that fascism is organically hysterical and there is no mild form of it—and I have met Negro college presidents whose notions are provocative of suspicious wonder and who, by the way they run "their" institutions, seem to be convinced that the methods of democracy are weak and decadent. Themselves, generally, victims of a tyranny imposed from without, they are tyrants within the academic group, and, if given a chance, outside it too. They play the strong man and the dictator role. They think that people and things should be "lined up" by the superior intellects with which they feel their positions endow them. They have a vast contempt for faculty members whom they regard as justly underprivileged employees perhaps of somewhat more value than janitors but of considerably less value than football coaches.

More dangerously, this presidential contempt engulfs students, who grow into maturity with personalities habituated to submission and who are likely to believe in the infallibility of the dictatorship principle. In general, Negro-educated Negroes have never learned to live with Freedom and this is why they are almost totally missing from the ranks of those who apply the privileges and the tools of democracy to the construction of Freedom's spacious house. Where they have taken over as leaders of Negro communities there rises a nauseating reek of devious and oily obsequiousness. It is a kind of fascism in reverse.

A group of Negro parents in a Virginia city wished to equalize the facilities of the Negro school with those of white schools. One of the things that the colored school lacked was a cafeteria. This was particularly noticeable because the city school board had just added such a convenience (at a cost of $20,000) to the only white school without it. The Negro parents went to the principal of their own school. As an ambitious and hard-working educator, less complacent and time-serving than most of his type, he had ideas, and the chief one was that the parents' group solicit funds (he thought $2,500 would do it!) in Negro homes, churches, and other racial institutions. By a show of initiative and energy, he thought, it might be brought home to the white people that Negro citizens were worthy of consideration.

Naturally among those to whom the project was first presented was the Negro acknowledged as the colored community's leader—a lawyer, graduate of a Negro college and a white law school. The esteem he commanded among his own people and the attention he could get from the whites were very real.

A friend of mine happened to be in the lawyer's office when the committee of parents went there. Whether out of boorishness, as my friend thinks, or because of the very human desire to prove his influence, or because he clearly saw his duty as a leader, the lawyer took over completely. "We'll get in touch with some real money," he said. "No point in piddling around with the colored folks' two cents' worth." Then, picking up the telephone, he called several of his white "friends"—a peanut-produce manufacturer (he carefully identified them between calls), a banker and an insurance broker, among others—and explained to them the Negro parents' project for the school. In ten minutes of "the most consummate fawning," my friend said afterward, the lawyer had solicited pledges of more than a thousand dollars. He typed out an identifying statement for the parents and sent them off to collect from his white friends.

My friend said she watched openmouthed during this masterly performance. "It was like being at the theater, when you're so struck by the skill of the star that you don't think of the play itself until after the curtain falls. Or maybe it isn't skill that strikes you. Maybe it's personality. I remember Katharine Cornell in—— Well, it was exactly like that," my friend said, with something very like awe in her voice and in her pale face. She recovered after the curtain had fallen.

"Mr. So-and-So," she asked, "do you mean to tell me you're begging white people in this community to give you things that everybody ought to have and that you have as much right to as they? This is 1951! Haven't you heard what's going on—the legal suits for equalization and all?"

"Oh," the lawyer said, laughing blandly, "they don't want to sue. They just want a cafeteria like the white schools have."

Thurgood Marshall, chief legal counsel of the National Association for the Advancement of Colored People, has said that the hardest job his staff has had in bringing equal-education suits has been to persuade Negro teachers and representative Negro parents to stand as plaintiffs. They have to be bludgeoned out of their childish faith in the short-term profits of their minority middle-class position. They have to be taught, with pain and patience, that democracy is a legitimate enterprise, that its institutions must make for their dignity, and that they cannot save themselves without forgetting themselves in the struggle to save the rights of man. Negro colleges are doing almost none of this teaching.*

What I am trying to make clear is the actual condition of the average middle-class American Negro mind halfway through the twentieth century. To explain how this condition came about would involve a good deal of history. Besides, I have already tried to explain it in another place. The only point is that the condition does exist, and it is not healthy. Nor can it be cured, it seems to me, by the superficial therapy of integration on special levels—the graduate and professional-school level, for instance—which is now being hailed as a cure-all. It is not. Integration on this level is at best a victory for the method of democracy, and method and spirit are not necessarily one. For years upper middle-class American Negroes have been going to graduate and professional schools with whites without learning, and without stimulating by their presence there, the inclusive kind of thinking that is necessary to the fulfillment of the spirit of democracy. Associations on such levels are as casual and random as the flow of unchanneled waters. They do not bite deep into idea patterns, nor thrust themselves down into the matrix of emotion.

Integration must start at much lower levels—in kindergarten and Sunday school, in Cub Scouts and Campfire Girls—before idea patterns are fixed and before the matrix of emotion is stuffed with the corruption of intolerance. Integration must be complete and absolutely without "ifs," "ands" and "buts." Eventually, of course, from these levels it would pro-

* Nor, it seems, are white colleges. Gordon Allport's study "Is Intergroup Education Possible?" (*Harvard Educational Review*, Vol. 15, No. 2), indicates that white college graduates, though more democratic than white high-school graduates, are not enough so to ensure the survival of democracy.

ceed to intermarriage. But what harm then? It is not entirely facetious to say that legal intermarriage would only sanction and somewhat equalize the miscegenation that has been going on in this country since 1622 when, it is said, the first child of mixed Negro-white parentage was born in America. And to say that intermarriage between American Negroes and whites would increase the vitality of the American people is biologically sound.

Fortunately integration is not a political concept (though it has been made a political issue) and is therefore not identified with the name of a leader. This has the advantage of depriving the opposition of that damaging leverage of vulnerable personality which leadership identification always provides and which can destroy or throw into long-lasting paralysis even the most salutary and easily defended social concepts. If you cannot overthrow the ideas which you fear or hate, then attack the man behind the ideas and thus debase what he stands for. That is the history of the struggle against ideas.

But if the concept of integration has this advantage, it has also the disadvantage of being indivisible. There is no decalogue of integration, each item of which can be separately assimilated and practiced. It is not a "one thing at a time" thing, nor a "first things first" thing. It must be assimilated all at once or killed all at once.

And it is this fact, I think, that frightens Negroes of the more stable classes. They see in integration a breakdown of certain monopolies in education and the professions and some business enterprises. In my own home town, for instance, where segregation could have been abolished twenty years ago, the Negro owner of the only Negro theater, who was at the same time on the city council, fought every attempt to wipe out the practice of excluding Negroes from white theaters, indoor sporting events, and other places of entertainment. He could get aid and comfort from a Negro school principal and certain Negro teachers who were afraid that the ell would lead to the mile and that their jobs would be thrown into an open nonracial competition which they were not prepared, they felt, to meet.

But also integration is in conflict with all that whites as well as Negroes have been taught to believe. It is in conflict with all that they think of as making for harmonious social development. Most whites are convinced that integration is the way to social and even biological disaster. Conviction is emotional and generally not to be argued with. If segregationalists could be argued with, they would not be segregationalists in the first place. They have taken their position on non-arguable grounds, and I think they have taken it quite contrary to their *intellectual* understanding of the problem central to our age. The Georgia Legislature, in this year 1951, was very sincere when it saw fit to pass a bill providing that no funds appropriated for education could go to institutions that did not enforce segregation. Only weeks later, Governor Byrnes of South Carolina, who has been a Senator, a Supreme Court Justice and Secretary of State, declared that "The politicians in Washington and the Negro agitators in North Carolina who today seek to abolish segregation in all schools will learn that what a carpetbag government could not do in the Reconstruction Period cannot be done in this period." He then proceeded to express the view that before what "could not be done" would be done, the public-school system in South Carolina would be abolished.°

° The quotations are from an Associated Press dispatch in the *New York Times* dated Columbia, S. C., January 24, 1951, and printed in the paper on January 25, 1951.

This is paradox and irony. There is the obvious irony of advocating the abolishment of the very thing on which democracy must rest—a publicly schooled citizenry—in order to ensure, as Byrnes implied, the perpetuation of democracy. But the paradox goes deeper, for if there is emotionalism in Byrnes's words, there is also the opposite of emotionalism. For his words represent a deliberate and a socially dominant response based on static concepts and ideals —the concept of the Negro's inherent inferiority, and the ideal of the white "Anglo-Saxon," predominantly Protestant community which earns its right to Divine favor because it contributes to Negro causes, does not deliberately encourage the persecution of either Jews or Catholics, and even occasionally permits itself the hazard of proclaiming the world one.

That the concept of complete integration, which seems to me to represent the logical evolution of democratic thinking, should be in deep conflict with the actualities of American learning (I will not say "teaching") is the supreme paradox of our democracy. The central problem of our age is that of expressing the oneness of man. The UNESCO "Statement on Race" makes this abundantly clear: "The unity of mankind from both the biological and social viewpoints is the main thing. To recognize this and to act accordingly is the first requirement of modern man." Admittedly Americans and a goodly portion of the peoples of the Western world believe that democracy is the frame—and perhaps the only frame— within which unity can be achieved and maintained. They must believe this, else their propagandic and materialistic promotion of it, their assiduous and even frantic efforts to "sell" it to the rest of the world is basically an immoral and selfish offering of the democratic experience to mankind at the price of man's soul. In so far as the American people, who lead the Western world, believe that democracy is the enduring frame of unity, then they must flatter themselves with a belief in a great destiny. And this is all very well, but they must also realize that Western democratic civilization has arrived at the point at which the path of development proper to man and necessary to democracy is marked "Integration." If it is not chosen now, then the American people must reform their wants, modify detrusively their ideals, and deliberately dissolve those organic bonds of principle which give the ultimate meaning to democracy. They must stop being moved by the symbols "the inalienable rights of man," "the pursuit of happiness," "liberty" and "equality," and enshrine, instead of these symbols of man's hope, those of fear—survival, collective security. The journey down the path of integration is not one to be put off until tomorrow. Tomorrow is now.

I do not wish to push this too far, but there can be little doubt that integration is a practical concern latent in our modern world. It is no preposterous idealism offered merely in contravention of a prevailing view and practices that are working for most men. The simple truth is that the prevailing practices are not working for most men. While at the same time his conscience is disturbed by this fact, Western man is so fixed in the once-comfortable conviction of his own superiority that he seems powerless to change the practices that support his conviction. This is a fault of his adolescence. It is a cavalier unconcern for his lack of knowledge of others. It is an inability to understand the world society of which he is a part. "World society" is no longer a metaphysical abstraction. It is very real, very concrete. It is real enough to have reduced the margin for national initiative in the conduct of internal affairs. It is no longer possible for the United States to keep the differences she has made between the races—and embedded in law and custom—without making a fundamental denial of what she professes before the world to stand for and to fight for, the entity of mankind.

12

PERHAPS I MAKE TOO MUCH OF THIS, and perhaps I am overwrought and unreasonable about it. I must confess that there flit across my mind, like stones skipped on the surface of water (only to sink into it), thoughts of my sons. There are moments when I am sentimental enough to hope that history is a necessary progress toward better things and that frustrations of the human spirit grow less and less. I know better. But I have such hopes when my sons are involved, and I am inclined to support them intemperately.

It does not serve merely to shrug one's shoulders and carp about the psychic traumas that bedevil American man. At least it did not do seven years ago, when my older son was eight and my younger not yet born. And now that my younger is himself almost seven, it still will not do. Argument does not exactly serve either, although I think I argue for something eminently sane. It is simplicity. I argue the substitution of spontaneous, instinctive responses for the deliberate responses based, as I have said above, on unchanging ideas and ideals. It seems to me that the old rules—evoked as they were out of the utmost confusion of morality and social expedience, and deliberate ignorance—are not only unnecessarily complicated for modern times and people, but that they are progressively unsuitable to modern ways of living, to the advance of knowledge, to technology, and (surely everyone will allow this) to one-worldness. Make the rules simple enough and we can play the hardest game.

What happened to my older son (and also to my younger son just recently, though not in circumstances so distressing nor in details so graphic) was that while he was playing the game with all the exuberance of an eight-year-old, somebody "complicated up" the rules. I remember distinctly how it happened.

For several weeks while my wife was with child it was my unaccustomed duty to "make the marketing," as it is so quaintly put in the upper South. Our market was a co-op on the highway just outside town, in the heart of one of those neat and monotonous residential communities that seemed to spring up everywhere in the 1940's. My wife loved the place. It was convenient; its stock was excellent; and its prices generally somewhat lower than in the chain groceries. Besides, it had a Negro (a colleague and friend) on its board of directors, and, as a second novel attraction, it employed several Negroes—at least one as clerk and another as butcher. The co-op's atmosphere, unlike that of the chain's, was friendly, warm, leisurely. My wife supposed it was because of the neighborhood—a better-than-average middle-class neighborhood, segregated of course, of aircraft designers, engineers and other technological experts and a scattering of armed-service personnel (no one lower than a lieutenant in the Navy or a captain in the Army, it seemed) from the various military installations close by. As one of the charter stockholders, I was determined to love the place too.

Friday was market day. Until her condition prevented her going, my wife's eager companion on these expeditions was our son. Sometime in the spring he

had struck up a friendship at the co-op and he antici-
pated its weekly renewal with pleasurable excitement. The first time I took him there I saw the re-
vival of the fraternity with quickened heart. My son
burst through the door ahead of me, stopped, looked
down the first aisle (fresh fruits and vegetables), ran
to the second and looked, and then suddenly let out
an Indian whoop—"Reggie!"—and got one for an answer—"Conway!" And then I saw a handsome dark-
haired, dark-eyed boy of about Conway's age break
from the side of a young Negro girl and come bursting up the aisle between the high-stacked shelves of
brightly packaged foods toward my son. They stood
looking at each other for a moment, then they came
together, each with an arm around the shoulder of
the other, and exploded off to play outside among the
cars until market was made. I looked at the uniformed Negro girl and she smiled and I smiled, and
that was that.

It was that way for four or five weeks—Conway and
Reggie met each other with what seemed the force of
projectiles and went skyrocketing off. Leaving the
market, I would find them outside, hot and happy
playing at some impossible game.

Then one Friday, Reggie (we never learned his last
name) was not there with the Negro maid. His guard-
ian this time was a man—a tall, handsome person,
about forty, I judged, who in spite of the Phi Beta
Kappa key slung across his flat stomach, looked out-
doorsy and virile. The boys came together as usual
and went outside as usual, but the man's marketing
must have been nearly done, for before I could
finish picking out the heaviest, juiciest oranges, Conway was back with me again. "Where's Reggie?" I
asked him. "He had to go," he said. "His daddy was in
a hurry." But already he was looking forward to
the next week.

The uniformed maid was with Reggie again the

next week, but this time when Conway let out his customary whoop, there was no vocal answer. Reggie turned, it seemed to me with momentary eagerness, but there was no yell and rush. He approached very slowly. He was smiling weakly, but that smile died as he came. Perhaps sensing that something was wrong, Conway himself now hesitated. "What's the matter?" he asked Reggie. "Come on, man, let's go. Don't you want to play?"

"I can't play with you," Reggie said.

"What's the matter, are you sick?" Conway wanted to know.

"I just can't play with you any more," Reggie said.

Conway moved a fraction closer to me, clutched the handle of the food cart I was pushing. The maid stood at some distance, pretending not to watch. The pleasant-voiced, pleasant-faced shoppers of the neighborhood flowed around us. Other children, younger, skittered and yelled up and down the aisles. The compacted odors of fresh pastry, of ground coffee, of fruits and vegetables. and the colors of all these were as ever. But a chill was beginning to form around my heart. Before Conway asked the next question, I knew the answer that was coming. I did not know the words of it, but I knew the feel—the iron that he would not be prepared for; the corrosive rust that it would make in his blood and that, unless I was skillful—as my father was not—I could never draw off. At that moment—no, before the moment of the answer I wanted to pick Conway up and hold him hard against me and ward off the demoralizing blow that might be struck for a lifetime. But I could not forfend it even by grasping my son by the hand and walking off in another direction. I was transfixed.

"Why?"

Reggie scowled then, a grimace that was not really ugly yet, because it was associated only with words and not with feeling. That would come later, and the word would be made flesh, and the flesh would be his forever. Now the scowl was only imitation.

"Because you're a nigger, that's why," Reggie said.

Conway looked at me wonderingly, not feeling hurt, as they say a man knowing himself shot but still without pain will look with surprise.

"I'm better than you," Reggie said, "'cause my father said so."

"You are not," Conway said, but I thought he shrank a little against me.

"No, son, he isn't," I said.

"I am so, too," Reggie said, looking at both of us. Words were beginning to arouse emotion and link with emotion. The sneer was no longer imitation. He stood bearing his weight on his left foot, his hands in the pockets of his khaki shorts, the whiteness of him showing in a streak just below the hairline, the rest of him—bare trunk, bare legs—tanned almost to the color of my son.

"No, son," I said, as much to the one as to the other. I think I felt sorry for Reggie too. I do now at any rate, thinking back.

"You are not," Conway said, and straightened. "My daddy says you aren't."

"You don't go to my school, you don't go to my church, you don't go to the movies I go to. I bet you never even seen Tim Holt," he put in parenthetically, "and that's because you're not good enough. Yah-yah!" Reggie said. "Niggers work for us, niggers work for us, you're a nigger and Trixie's a nigger and Trixie works for us." It was a shrilling singsong. "Yah-yah nigger nigger, go peddle your papers, nigger!" With this he ran off, back, I suppose, to Trixie, who worked for him because she was a nigger.

Conway did not cry, but in his eyes was the look of a wound, and I knew how it could grow, become infected and pump its poison to every tissue, to every brain cell. He stayed close to me while I made market. On the way home, he said savagely, "I hate this car!"

It did not seem like any kind of entree to what I knew I must talk about, and the sooner the better. When what happened to him happens it makes a nasty wound which demands immediate attention. You want a knife to do the job quickly, deftly, cleanly, but the only instruments in the surgery kit are words.

So when I wanted to know what was wrong with the car and why he hated it, and he said, "Why can't we have a good car, a new one with a radio, and a bigger one—like Reggie's?" I tried to explain to him that it was wartime, that cars were scarce and prices high, and that in order to get a new car you had to do something a little underhanded, something that was not much different from stealing or cheating.

"Did Reggie's father steal?"

"I wouldn't say that," I said, "but I wouldn't put it past him. He's not a good man."

"How do you know? You don't know him, do you?"

"No," I said, "but I don't have to know him to know he's not a good man." I put it as simply as I could. I told him that parents are frequently reflected in their children. I made him laugh a little by reminding him of the time, when he was six, he had acutely embarrassed his mother and me by telling one of our friends, "I think you have store-bought teeth," which was exactly what he had heard me say about the friend.

"Those things Reggie said today, his father said to him. That's how I know Reggie's father is not a good man."

"He wasn't telling the truth, was he?"

"No," I said, shaking my head.

"I mean about him being better?"

"No," I answered.

"Then why can't I go to his school and to his movies?"

This was the deeper infection, and I did not know how to deal with it. Words were poultices to seal the infection in. I could recall them from my own childhood in answer to a "why?" For children are not born with answers. Words spoken by my parents, my teachers, my friends. Words could seal in the infection and seal in also the self that might never break through again except with extreme luck. But I had no choice save to use them. I told him about prejudice. No one has ever made the anatomy of prejudice simple enough for children.

"And the reason you don't go to Reggie's school," I remember saying, "is because there are people like Reggie's father."

"It's all complicated up," Conway answered.

It was a relief to laugh at his child's expression, but I noticed he was not laughing, and at home some minutes later, when I had finished storing the groceries in the pantry, I found him pressed against his mother's rounded bosom crying without restraint. But even that did not end it. "He cried it all out," his mother said. She was wrong.

Seven years afterward, in the late spring of 1950, we had a letter from the headmaster of Conway's New England preparatory school: "We have been unable to reach him. . . . He seems to prefer to be alone and will not participate even in those activities for which he has undoubted talents. Naturally this attitude has given us serious concern, for an important part of our educational program is training in citizenship and co-operative living. . . ."

Perhaps there is only a slight connection, but I would be hard to convince.

13

I AM WELL AWARE THAT THERE IS supposed to be something reprehensible in advocating marriage between races—enough, were I a faculty member in a public-supported college in the South, to bring about my dismissal for advocacy of it. In some metaphysical corner of the white man's mind intermarriage is identified with immorality, biological peculiarity and perversion. This identification is partly a matter of conscience and, as Gunnar Myrdal exhaustively explains, partly a matter of jealousy. The unrestricted use of the Negro woman as sex mate and mammy during slavery did a strange thing to the white man's mind. It filled it with anxiety, guilt, and a grotesque exaggeration of the Negro male's sexual equipment—an equipment from which the white male has felt compelled to protect white womanhood ever since. In Myrdal's words, "The necessity to 'protect' the white female against this fancied prowess of the male Negro [is] a fixed constellation in the ethos" of America.

The common belief runs that the white girl who marries a Negro is morally depraved and certainly sexually abnormal, for no *normal* white woman could possibly enjoy the average Negro's savage sexual potency. As for the white man who marries a Negro woman, he will soon "tire of her extraordinary sensuality and return to the safer, saner sex practices" of his own kind. Such assertions, made by the majority race with all the blatant insistence of an uneasy conscience, have conditioned the Negro sufficiently to prevent his speaking out in favor of intermarriage. But no one has bothered to validate the declarations of sexual incompatibility between the races with scientific investigations. (No one, so far as I know, has made a study, for instance, of the comparative sexuality of the Negro American and the white American.) That such incompatibility exists between normal individuals of the two races is an emotion-based assumption which finds sanction and support in statutes prohibiting intermarriage. Such statutes seem to me to be the most fundamental expression of the human inequality to which the Negro is subjected. They strike at the deepest roots of personal dignity and self-respect. It is one thing, and a very good thing, to be acknowledged as a first-class citizen: it is another and a better thing to be acknowledged a first-class human being. This is the ultimate civility.

But if the assumption of sexual incompatibility is based in emotion, the beliefs about miscegenation are founded on pure mythology. The myths about Negro-white blood mixture are a curious interweaving of the biological, the moral and the social. The myths are contradictory enough to be mutually exclusive, but emotionalism absorbs the contradictions. In the first place, quite contrary to all other blood-group designations, in America anyone having a single drop of Negro blood is classed as a Negro. In as much as this practice was thought to place a restraint on inter-racial concubinage (though during slavery its real purpose was to increase the number of human chattels), it once had a kind of left-handed moral sanction. Since that time it has become a national habit and is solidified by law in the Southern states. It has engendered beliefs as irrational and as inexplicable as nightmares.

White men have won libel suits for mistakenly being called Negro, yet there is a strong belief among the majority of whites that for the Negro to have white blood is to adulterate his highest and best potentials. But the matter is even crazier than that, for another belief is simultaneously held: only Negroes with white blood begin to approach the white man's biological, mental and moral standards. At the same time that the Rev. Thomas Dixon, Jr., was setting forth in his best-selling novel (*The Leopard's Spots*) and his smash-hit drama (*The Clansman*) the proposition that the offspring of mixed parentage were degenerate, crafty, vicious and depraved, the superior attainments of Booker T. Washington were being accounted for by the fact that his father was white. The kind, gentle, loyal Negro mammies were always pure black; but all the colored tarts that ever lured white men to Lethean beds were "high yaller."

The term "half white," forever loosely used, covers all degrees of blood mixture and all kinds of contrarieties. If there were rationality in the matter, then in keeping with the implication of the dominance of Negro blood over white blood in the accepted definition of Negro, the term would be "half black." It makes no kind of sense that "half white" should mean an endowment of all the criminal tendencies *and* a prodigy like Philippa Schuyler (whose mother is white) and Walter White (who is more than a quarter white) and the novelist Frank Yerby (who is perhaps an eighth) and Ralph Bunche (who is a thirty-second). It makes no kind of sense that an intelligent white woman on first seeing Paul Robeson, whose reputation was international and then unsmirched, should remark to her companion, "Why, I expected him to be black! I thought, you know, if they had white blood they generally turned out badly."

If that were the case, at least ten million of the fourteen million American Negroes would be bad ones. And if all those who have a drop of Negro blood confessed to it, there would be uncountable numbers more. For the fact is that many miscegenates pass over into the white race every day. A conservative estimate is that four million Negroes, with all their spermatozoa and ova, genes and chromosomes, have been absorbed into the white American blood stream in the last two decades. They have left scarcely a trace. Negroes throw up a protective wall of silence around individual passing. Thus it is well known among colored people that a certain famous moving picture star is the daughter of a Negro woman. The white but not the Negro public was shocked four or five years ago when a prominent New York lawyer made a courtroom confession of his tar-brushed parentage in order to clear himself for a share in a rich bequest. Many "white" people eminent in public life, in industry, in government, and the arts are known by Negroes to be Negro.

And if there were truth in the myths, passing would be all but impossible. The black blood would tell in real life as it is so frequently made to do in fiction. Industrialists and other employers would detect it in absenteeism, gold-bricking and general shiftlessness. Psychologists would spot it by behavior indexes—unmodulated speech, flashy clothes and other forms of exhibitionism. Physiologists would detect it in the shape and tincture of the fingernails and in the thickness of the skull. Anatomists would see it in "the curious heel structure" (which was supposed to account for the speed of Jesse Owens, Ralph Metcalfe, *et al.!*) of the Negro male and in the peculiar "ovoid shape of the [Negro] female's buttocks." * Psychiatrists would mark it in overt aggressive tendencies, or in other forms of emotional infantilism, or in a total absence of emotional response. And everyone would detect it in the "rusty," "acrid," "unbearable" odor that Negroes give off.

* Quoted from John H. Van Evrie's *White Supremacy and Negro Subordination; or, Negroes a Subordinate Race* (1867).

14

WHILE I AM IN A PETULANT MOOD,
let me say that I am race-conscious enough to be
shocked and irritated frequently by what even professed white friends do not know, on both the personal and historical level, about Negroes. There is a
glaring case in point.

During her husband's administration, Mrs. Eleanor
Roosevelt became acquainted with a black, bosomy
and intensely dynamic woman named Mrs. Mary Mc-
Leod Bethune. The Negro woman was then Deputy
Administrator of NYA, and through her the President's wife, a sincere and fearless woman, got closely
involved with the race problem. The white South
fretted over the spectacle of Mrs. Roosevelt being
shepherded through the intricate mazes of racial and
interracial affairs. It was alleged (and the South, as
did Negroes everywhere, took it for truth) that Mrs.
Bethune, through Mrs. Roosevelt, had special rights
to the President's ear. She certainly seemed to have
such rights to the ear of F.D.R.'s wife. More than
one photograph shows the two women in earnest
conversation in what seem to be intimate circumstances.

Mrs. Bethune is very much alive. She is frequently
mentioned and pictured in the colored press. She is
ex-president of the National Federation of Colored

Women. She took a dominant part in a conference on old age at the Shoreham Hotel in Washington in 1950. She spoke at perhaps a half dozen major college commencements in 1951. But in her book *This I Remember*, written in 1949, Mrs. Roosevelt, after words of heartening warmth for the black woman, refers to her as "the late [dead, deceased!] Mrs. Mary McLeod Bethune." Mrs. Roosevelt's reputation (earned at the cost of great personal criticism) for knowledge about and interest in Negroes, for liberalism, for social intelligence and tact is as a broad pen stroke underscoring the pattern of false belief and cavalier know-nothing-about-the-Negro attitude to which the majority conforms. Yet even she could make this error!

As an ideal, of course, I am all for the deletion of racial designations in newspaper stories and the like. But the ideal is nowhere near attainment. It seems that it is still a general practice in newsrooms in a large part of the country to specify race when Negroes are involved in crime, and it is still usual to omit, except from feature stories and special articles, racial designation in news copy that would reflect credit on the colored people. When Ralph Bunche stepped in as mediator of the Jewish-Arab dispute, the fact that he was an American Negro first broke in the foreign press. In spite of hundreds of front-page news stories from competent war correspondents, it is even now not generally known that the 24th Infantry, which fought so hard and bought with its life (it was almost totally destroyed) the time General MacArthur needed in the early fighting in Korea, was a Negro outfit in the segregated United States Army.

Personally, as matters stand, I would settle for something less than the ideal. Seldom does one see the minority-group designations "Italian," "Greek," "Jewish," "Irish," and the like attached to crime stories involving persons of these groups. But neither, it is replied, do you see them attached to other stories. True, and this is all very well. It is a matter of nomenclature. Negro names being what they generally are—as indigenous to America as "hot dog," or as unmistakably Anglo-Saxon-derived as "Gudger"— Ralph Bunche and Charles Drew, William Hastie and George Dows Cannon might belong to any Anglo-Saxon, Protestant or Catholic. But no one of reading intelligence would mistake Bernard Baruch or Sholem Asch as of other than Jewish heritage, or Fiorello La-Guardia and Vincent Impellitteri as of other than Italian ancestry, or George Skouras as of other than Greek, or Roosevelt and Vanderbilt as other than Dutch, or William Cardinal O'Connell as other than Irish. We make these associations automatically, and there passes into the communal intelligence some sense of the contributions these groups make to American life. On the other hand, diffused throughout our national life and thought is the fallacy that the Negro has contributed nothing substantial.

Not to know the Negro on the group and historical level is to rob him of his pride and of his rightful share in the American heritage. He cannot claim what is his, except in an intorted and psychologically unhealthy way. The Negro on the lower levels saves himself from complete madness by following a pattern of neurotic expression that is patent in his lazy-lipped and mumbling speech, in his gay-bird dress, and in his prowllike walk. The Negro on the upper level turns back upon himself with a voracity of egocentrism that bewilders the casual observer. "What a self-conscious people your Negroes are!" a recent French visitor exclaimed. He was right. The Negro lives constantly on two planes of awareness. Watching the telecast of a boxing match between Ezzard Charles, the Negro who happened to be heavyweight champion, and a white challenger, a friend of mine said, "I don't like Charles as a person [one level] but I've got to root for him to beat this white boy—and good [second level]."

One's heart is sickened at the realization of the primal energy that goes undeflected and unrefined into the sheer business of living as a Negro in the United States—in any one of the United States. Negroness is a kind of superconsciousness that directs thinking, that dictates action, and that perverts the expression of instinctual drives which are salutary and humanitarian—the civic drive, for instance, so that in general Negroes are cynically indifferent to politics; the societal drive. so that ordinarily the Negro's concern is only with himself as an individual; and even the sex and love drive, so that many Negroes suffer sexual maladjustments and many a Negro couple refuse to bear children who will "inevitably grow up under a burden of obloquy and shame that would daunt and degrade a race of angels." It is impossible to believe with Lillian Smith that the psychological damage caused by the race situation in America is greater to whites than to Negroes. "Every one of us knows," an internationally known Negro said recently, "that there is no 'normal' American Negro." Public asylums for the mentally deranged offer a telling statistic. Though Negroes are something less than ten per cent of the country's population, they are eleven per cent of the total population of public institutions for the insane.

Compulsively dissociated from the American tradition, the Negro on the upper level has had to maintain the pretense of possessing what he is in fact denied. He has had no choice but this. He has not been free to realize his ideals or to strive to be what the American tradition has made him wish to be. Paul Lawrence Dunbar, probably the most popular American poet at the turn of the century, did not wish to write "jingles in a broken tongue," but he was Negro and as a Negro he had to write dialect or else have no hearing as a poet. James Weldon Johnson did not wish to compose those "darky" lyrics and "coon songs" for Williams and Walker's and his own brother Rosamond's shows—nor did Williams and Walker and Rosamond Johnson wish to sing them and caper to them. But how else were they to find outlets for their creative urges, when all of the more congenial and less particularized were dammed up against them? DuBois had ideas for a career other than the one he was compelled to follow. "Had it not been for the race problem early thrust upon me and enveloping me," he wrote in *Dusk of Dawn*, "I should have probably been an unquestioning worshiper at the shrine of the social order and economic development into which I was born. . . . What was wrong was that I and people like me and thousands of others who might have my ability and aspiration, were refused permission to be a part of this world. It was as though moving on a rushing express, my main thought was as to the relations I had to other passengers on the express, and not to its rate of speed and its destination. . . . My attention from the first was focused . . . upon the problem of the admission of my people into the freedom of democracy." *

The dissociation of the Negro from the American tradition and the lack of knowledge of the Negro on the historical level are certainly in part the fault of social commentators and historians and social scholars. The historians particularly have been guilty of almost complete silence, like William A. Dunning; or of faulty investigation, like James Ford Rhodes; or of misinterpretation of the facts, like Ulrich Philips and W. E. Woodward; or of propaganda, like William E. Dodd and Jesse Carpenter; or of frank and

* W. E. B. DuBois, *Dusk of Dawn* (New York: Harcourt, Brace and Company, 1940), pp. 27-28. Reprinted by permission of the publishers.

determined anti-Negro bias, like dozens, major and minor, including Claude Bowers, James Truslow Adams, and John W. Burgess—the last of whom, by his prestige as a faculty member at Columbia University, gave scholarly sanction to prejudice. He wrote as follows:

"The claim that there is nothing in the color of the skin from the point of view of political ethics is a great sophism. A black skin means membership in a race of men which has never of itself succeeded in subjecting passion to reason, has never, therefore, created any civilization of any kind. To put such a race of men in possession of a 'state' government in a system of federal government is to trust them with the development of political and legal civilization upon the most important subjects of human life. . . . There is something natural in the subordination of an inferior race to a superior race, even to the point of the enslavement of the inferior race. . . . It is the white man's mission, his duty and his right, to hold the reins of political power in his own hands for the civilization of the world and the welfare of mankind." [*]

Ignorance and willful distortion of the facts of American life and history in regard to the Negro's role have set the Negro scholar what up to now has been a thankless task. In pure self-defense he has had to try to set the record straight. The first Negro professional writer in America, William Wells Brown, was primarily a historian. Negro scholars have written thousands of dissertations, theses, monographs, articles, essays and books in a gigantic effort to correct the multiple injuries done the race by white writers. Five great collections—at Howard, Hampton, Fisk, Yale, and the Harlem Branch of the New York

[*] John W. Burgess, *Reconstruction and the Constitution* (New York: Charles Scribner's Sons, 1903), p. 133. Reprinted by permission of the publishers.

Public Library—house thousands of volumes and hundreds of magazine and newspaper files, but few except Negroes bother to disturb their dust. Whites show little interest in this Negroana. They seem to feel that they do not need to know about the Negro; they seem to feel that the basic truths about him were established long ago. Even the primary source material on him whom white America calls the greatest Negro American, him whom they have enshrined in the Hall of Fame and about whom they have written ten million words—even the primary source material on Booker Washington—some twenty thousand letters and other papers—remain scarcely touched and certainly unexplored in the Library of Congress, though the Harvard University Press published an erudite and "definitive biography" of the man in 1949.

Negro writers remain generally unrepresented in anthologies of American literature, though in the light of the cultural history of America, the slave biographies (and there are some "literary" ones among them) are at least as important as anything Seba Smith, Charles Augustus Davis, John P. Kennedy and William Gilmore Simms ever wrote. Paul Lawrence Dunbar was a better poet, and, in the opinion of William Dean Howells, a more popular poet and, by the very standard of indigenousness which some anthologists claim to follow, a more important poet than James Whitcomb Riley. James Weldon Johnson and Claude McKay enjoyed international reputations as writers, but they are absent from the best-known American anthologies. Richard Wright has been translated into a dozen languages, including the Chinese, and is rated by Europeans with Steinbeck, Hemingway and Faulkner, but American anthologies neglect him. Gwendolyn Brooks has won the Pulitzer prize for poetry, which is more than Jesse Stuart and William Carlos Williams have done, but her work is not in the collections of American writing.

Nor is the most representative work by whites who have written about Negroes with some regard for justice and truth. Editors use Faulkner's "A Rose for Emily," "The Bear" and chapters from *Sartoris* and *Told by an Idiot,* but not "Evening Sun Go Down," or excerpts from *Light in August* and *Intruder in the Dust.* Chapters from *Huckleberry Finn* are used, but not those which show Nigger Jim to be much like other human beings, nor those which excoriate the institution of slavery and express Huck's hatred of it. George W. Cable is generally represented by selections from *Old Creole Days* and innocuous passages from *The Grandissimes,* but never by *Madame Delphine* (certainly one of his best books), *The Silent South* or *The Negro Question.*

The result of this arrogant neglect has been to render American cultural history less effective as an instrument of diagnosis and evaluation. What we have as history reflects little credit upon American historians as scholars. Their work makes pleasant reading and inflates the national ego, but it does not tell those sometimes hard and shameful truths that might now be helpful for the world to know. What Lillian Smith calls "the old conspiracy of silence" needs to be broken, and the "maze of fantasy and falsehood that [has] little resemblance to the actual world" needs to be dissolved. The psychopathic resistance to self-knowledge that the American mind has developed must be broken down. What we have got to know are the things that actually happened—and are still happening—in America. With these things clear before us, perhaps we can use our knowledge and experience for the guidance of mankind.

15

BUT THERE ARE LIMITS TO WHAT EVEN knowledge can accomplish, as any psychologist will tell you. Knowledge alone is not enough to redeem life from folly and to save men from despair. If it ever was, it is no longer valid to assume that learning's supreme glory is in the safeguarding of humanity, the dispelling of prejudice, and the achieving of those moral values that are said to have inspired men of other ages. Perhaps I am deeply pessimistic, but I simply cannot believe that if only people knew enough of the what, the why and the how, all would be right with the world. Knowledge does not ensure moral behavior; it all too willingly puts itself at the service of despotism and inhumanity. I suppose that what is lacking in our modern learning and among our modern learned is a sense that morality is the product of human experience—that it comes, anciently out of a wisdom we have forgotten, from a realization of the character of human life.

Certainly the moralistic approach to human relations in general and to race relations in particular in America has failed so consistently that one mentions this approach with embarrassment and reluctance. It is considered namby-pamby, pusillanimous, Uncle-Tomish. Few, even of the ministers of the gospel, appeal to nobility and virtue and goodness any more, except as these qualities seem disingenuously to be connected with "practical concerns." We no longer think of great men as being great in those virtuous qualities to which former and simpler ages subscribed. Those moral excellencies—love, honor, truth—seem to many ordinary people "a long way removed from our normal affairs." Great men today are "practical-minded," "realistic" and "public-spirited," and none of these attributes, I take it, is necessarily virtuous. To be trite about it, any one of them can cover a multitude of evils. The realistic attitude has been the excuse for innumerable travesties of human rights; in the name of public spirit heinous crimes have been committed against the dignity of man; and too many politicians and diplomats have made practical-mindedness the inviolable sanction for the suppression of the worthy ambitions of the powerless.

It must be, for instance, the operation of these qualities that is leading to the continuing farce that American men are making of UNESCO's Universal Declaration of Human Rights. They are making a farce of both its purpose and its content. Everyone knows—or certainly everyone should know—what the Universal Declaration of Human Rights is. It is a document so clearly and simply expressive of what is in the hearts and minds of the men of the masses that, indeed, a man of the masses might easily have written it. In 1946, the representatives of eighteen national governments—members of the United Nations —began work on the framing of a statement that would, as Mrs. Eleanor Roosevelt said, "establish standards for human rights and freedom the world over," so that the recognition of these rights and freedoms "might become one of the corner-stones on which peace could eventually be based." Two years later the Commission on Human Rights presented its declaration to the General Assembly of the United Nations. Forty-eight governments voted to accept it.

What they voted to accept is stated in the preamble:

"Whereas recognition of the inherent dignity and of the equal and inalienable rights of all members of the human family is the foundation of freedom, justice and peace in the world,

"Whereas disregard and contempt for human rights have resulted in barbarous acts which have outraged the conscience of mankind, and the advent of a world in which human beings shall enjoy freedom of speech and belief and freedom from fear and want has been proclaimed as the highest aspiration of the common people. . . .

"Whereas the peoples of the United Nations have in the Charter reaffirmed their faith in fundamental human rights, in the dignity and worth of the human person and in the equal rights of men and women and have determined to promote social progress and better standards of life in larger freedom. . . ."

This was fine and hopeful, and, indeed, the more so that the Declaration was born of the Charter of the United Nations. The Charter is no blueprint for an abstract world. It sets a premium on maturity, of course; but also it sets a premium on respect for reality.

After the General Assembly's acceptance, to make the Universal Declaration law there remained only the act of ratification by each participating government. It was at this point that a hitch developed. Perhaps the State Department had dismissed, even at its inception, the work of the Commission on Human Rights as unimportant. Perhaps the State Department was so concerned with the "practical and immediate" problems of the cold war that it simply forgot the Declaration for two years, and forgot, too, that the United States had taken the lead in securing the General Assembly's adoption of a resolution embodying the Declaration. Perhaps there were petty and selfish political considerations. Perhaps there was bald hypocrisy in the whole thing. I cannot give cause. I can only declare that when, in 1950, after what seemed an unnecessarily long delay, the matter of ratification by the United States came up, the State Department demurred.

At first it demurred over the inclusion of Articles 22-27 of the Declaration. But since most of these articles embody principles which are already written into United States law or supported by immemorial custom, the State Department's objection to them seemed inexplicable. As Rayford Logan, a member of the United States National Commission for UNESCO, pointed out at the time, there is nothing revolutionary to American principles in the statement that "Everyone . . . has a right to social security," or in the statement that "Everyone has a right to education," or in the statement that "Everyone has the right to a standard of living adequate for health." No. The objection seemed to be to Article 23:

"(1) Everyone has the right to work, to *free* choice of employment, to just and favorable conditions of work and to protection against unemployment. (2) Everyone, *without any discrimination*, has the right to equal pay for equal work. . . ." (Italics mine.)

Once the Declaration was ratified, these clauses would have necessitated the establishment of a law no different in intent from the proposed F.E.P.C. But this is not the point that Mr. Edward W. Barrett, of the State Department, made in stating the objection to acceptance of the entire declaration. "Whereas," he wrote, "a maximum degree of agreement exists (outside the Iron Curtain) on political and civil rights, there is no general agreement on economic and social rights. The laws and practices of the members of the United Nations differ widely on those rights as set forth in the Declaration."

It does not particularly matter, I suppose, that this amounts to saying that the United Nations had not agreed on what they obviously had agreed on; nor that no clear and sharp distinction (such as Mr. Barrett's letter implies) can be drawn between political and civil rights on the one hand and economic and social rights on the other.

It does not particularly matter because the State Department gave even grosser expression to the "realistic" point of view that, to paraphrase, democracy is based on compromises in which big ends are surrendered to small goals. Article 16 of the Universal Declaration of Human Rights says:

"(1) Men and women of full age, *without any limitation due to race*, nationality or religion, have the right to marry and to found a family. . . ." (Italics mine.)

Could it be that this provision was in Mr. Barrett's mind when he wrote: "Neither the Executive Branch nor the Congress would desire that our Government should ratify a convention which contains obligations that our Government and our people are unwilling or unable to honor." ?

There is a deep sickness in the American mind and spirit, and it threatens to infect democracy itself and render it impotent as an ideal. But not only this; the sickness also threatens to make democracy ineffective as an instrument through which the individual can realize his highest self and in co-operation with other selves give zest, richness and meaning to human endeavor. For democracy is two things. It is a political instrument: it is an ideal. As an ideal, the notion of the world as a vast arena, where purposeless and inexplicable forces play, and where inevitable fate renders the mind and the spirit of the individual helpless, dissolves before it. As an ideal, it is in raw conflict with sterile determinism and fatalism. It assumes that the only source of human happiness or misery is human beings themselves, and its very dogma proclaims that co-operative endeavor is the way to human happiness. And this is sensible, for we know—and we know it scientifically—that co-operation is the law of life. When men co-operate, they and their enterprises prosper; peace reigns. This is not humanistic nonsense. Authorized to speak the considered opinion of a group of renowned scientific scholars of the Committee of Experts on Race Problems of UNESCO, Ashley Montagu declared: "Man's *inherent* drives toward co-operation need but to be cultivated and intelligently handled for this world to be turned into a Paradise on earth—when all men will, at last, *live by the rule it is their nature to live by*—the Golden Rule to love your neighbor as yourself." (Italics mine.)

16

ALTHOUGH I AM NOT A VERY RE-
ligious person, I do not see how I can leave God out
of consideration in these matters. God has been made
to play a very conspicuous part in race relations in
America. At one time or another, and often at the
same time, He has been the protagonist for both sides.
He has damned and blessed first one side and then the
other with truly godlike impartiality. His ultimate
intentions, revealed to inspired sages, are preserved
in a thousand volumes. Anyone who reads the literature of race cannot but be struck by the immoderate
frequency with which God is invoked, and by the
painstaking consideration that is given, even by social
scientists, to race relations as a problem of Christian
ethics.

God, of course, is an implicit assumption in the
thought of our age. He is one of those beliefs so spontaneous and ineluctable and taken so much as a
matter of course that they operate with great effec-
tiveness (though generally on a level of subconscious-
ness) in our society. He is a belief that operates just
by being, like a boulder met in the path which must
be dealt with before one can proceed on his journey. God is a complex composed entirely of simple
elements—mediator, father, judge, jury, executioner,
and also love, virtue, charity—each of which gener-

ates a very motley collection of often contradictory ideas. God is a catalyst, and He is also a formulated doctrine inertly symbolized in the ritual and the dogma of churches called Christian. God is the Absolute Reality, but this does not prevent His being ostentatiously offered as the excuse for our society's failure to come to grips with big but relative realities. God and the Christian religion must be reckoned with.

I do not know how long I have held both God and the Christian religion in some doubt, though it must have been since my teens. Nor do I know exactly how this came about. My father was (and is) very religious, of great and clear and unbending faith. My mother was less so, but the family went regularly to church, where we were all active, and I used occasionally to see my mother so deeply touched by a religious feeling that she could not keep back the tears. What inspired it in that chill atmosphere it is impossible to say. I can only think that it came as a result of some very personal communion with God, established perhaps by a random thought, a word, or a certain slant of light through the yellow and rose and purple windows. There was never any shouting or "getting happy" among us, or in our church; none of that ecstatic abandon that set men and women jumping and dancing and screaming in the aisles. After the northward migration following the First World War, a few people who may have had a natural tendency to such transports found their way to our church, but they were frustrated by the mechanical expertness of the uninspired sermons, the formalized prayers, and by the choirmaster's preference for hymns translated from fifteenth-century Latin. Never did I hear a spiritual sung in our church, and only rarely a common-meter Calvinist hymn.

Sometime during my teens I became aware that for most Negroes God was a great deal more than a spirit to be worshiped on Sundays. He had a terrifying immediacy as material provider and protector. Once a group of us teen-agers went on a Sunday evening (our own church worshiped only in the morning) to a mission church deep in the Bridge District where the Negro population was concentrated. We went to mock, as some of us had heard our parents do, at the malapropisms of the illiterate minister and his ignorant flock, the crazy singing and shouting, and the uninhibited behavior of members in religious ecstasy. We did not remain to pray, but I was struck by what I saw and heard, and afterward my natural curiosity led me to go occasionally alone. The service did not resemble, either in ritual or content (both of which were created spontaneously), the service to which I was used. Any member of the church could stand up and pray. A whole evening might be given over to these impulsive outbursts. The prayers impressed me with their concreteness, their concern for the everyday. I heard one distraught mother, whose daughter evidently was sitting beside her, beseech God: "Now here's Idabelle, an' she's gone and got herself bigged, an' I'm askin' you, God, to make the young rascal who done it marry her. His name's Herbie Washington, an' he stays on the street nex' to me." They prayed for bread, not in a general, symbolic "give us this day our daily bread" sense, but for specific bread and meat for specific occasions. "Aunt Callie Black's laying up there sick, Lord, an' when I seen her, she tol' me her mouth was watering for some hot biscuit, an' that's the reason I'm asking You to give her some hot biscuit 'fore I go to see her again nex' Tuesday." They wanted clothes and they asked for them. They wanted pitiful but specific sums of money. They wanted protection from their real enemies. "Lord Jesus, don't let that mean nigger, Joe Fisher, stick me with no knife."

Negroes made irrational claims on God which they expected Him to fulfill without any help from them and without any regard for the conditions under which they could be fulfilled, and I suppose that when their claims failed, there was some sort of psychological mechanism that produced satisfactory excuses. It was all very simple and direct, but God just did not work that way—not the white folk's God I was taught to worship.

I do not believe that this incongruity set me thinking until at the small and rather exclusive (though public) high school I attended, a science teacher pointed it up. He was a bitter, frustrated man, full of self-hatred and of contempt for his race. Often staggering drunk outside the classroom, he was said to spend his week ends in an alcoholic fog of hatred writing scurrilous anti-Negro letters to the "people's opinion" column of the local paper. (Such letters did appear there with persistent regularity.) Our science teacher was certainly no good for us. Monday mornings were invariably void of science instruction.

"How many of you went hat-in-hand to God yesterday and asked him to get your chemistry for you this week?" he would begin. "He won't, and you can take my word for that. The trouble with niggers—" what malevolent contempt he put into the word!—"is that they look to God to do for them. That's why they're like they are—not only ignorant, but stupid; not only inferior, but debased. 'You can take all this world, but give me Jesus,' the song says, and that's just what the white people have been doing— taking the world and giving you Jesus. God, if there is a God, which I doubt, helps those who help themselves. Now study your chemistry!"

(How he managed to stay on with his drunkenness and his fundamental corruption, of which everyone was aware, is not beyond my comprehension so much as it is beyond my belief. He was one of the "big," upper-class mulatto families with members thriving in the professions up and down the Eastern seaboard.

They were not a powerful family, having neither money, nor political influence, nor potent white patrons; but they had social prestige because of their antiquity, their relatively long tradition of freedom, their education, and their considerable infusion of white blood. In those days the feeling was that such a family must not be disgraced by the derelictions of one of its members. The black sheep must be protected, if he could not be hidden, and pitied because he could not be punished.)

Such assertions were almost daily fare. It was not hard to find support for them. I could see that most Negroes were poor and ignorant and inferior. Every year on the last Sunday in August one of the Negro religious denominations held a "quarterly meeting" in my home town. People from a half dozen states poured in the day before and roamed the streets all night, or slept anywhere they could—on the courthouse lawn, in the wagons and trucks that brought them, in alleys and doorways. But on the Sunday, what excitement! What noisy exuberance! Six city blocks, just below the main street, were inundated with the germinal tide of their living. Preachers exhorted; food vendors shouted; choirs sang; bands played; lost children bawled; city prostitutes pushed brazenly for trade among the young men from the country; people prayed and went into transports.

I do not know when I began to notice the white people. I suppose they had always been there. But along in my fourteenth or fifteenth year, I suddenly seemed to see them. Small phalanxes of them always seemed to be pushing or imperiously demanding passage through the crowds that fell away before them like grain before a scythe. The white people sneered —or so it seemed to me—and took pictures and made derisive comments. They looked down in laughing contempt from the windows, balconies and roofs of the buildings that lined the street. They came, also from miles around, to watch the show, not to be a part of it. I realized with deep shame that what the Negroes did on this holy day made a clowns' circus for the whites. The Negroes' God made fools of them. Worship and religiosity were things to be mocked and scorned, for they stamped the Negro as inferior.

There must have been many vague progressions of thought and many gradations of emotion between the premise and the conclusion. However little I was aware of them, my nerves, muscles and brain—conditioned by a thousand random and forgotten experiences—must have prepared me to accept the conclusion without outrage and shock. I simply rejected religion. I rejected God. Not my instincts, but my deepest feelings revolted compulsively—not because I was I, a sort of neutral human stuff reacting directly to experience, but because I was Negro. It is hard to make it clear; but there were two people sharing my physical existence and tearing me apart. One, I suppose, was the actual self which I wanted to protect and yet which I seemed to hate with a consuming hatred; and the other was the ideal self which tried compulsively to shape the actual self away from all that Negroes seemed to be. At what emotional and psychic cost this deep emotional conflict went on within me I do not know. It was years before I understood that what I had wanted then was to be white.

It was also years before I made a sort of armed truce with religion and with God. I stepped around God determinedly, gingerly, gloating that I was free of Him and that He could not touch me. Indeed, I had to step around Him, for He was always there. He was there, foursquare and solid, at the very center of my father's life. (My father habitually ends his letters, "May the spirit of the Almighty God, whose interest is always manifest, be with you!") At Brown University He was in Dr. Washburn's sermons, and

President Faunce's chapel talks, and Professor Ducasse's philosophy course. He was in various people I met and felt affection for. He was in the ineffable, tremulous sweetness of the first love I felt; in the drowning ecstasy of the first sexual experience; in the joy of imaginative creation. But I moved around Him warily, laughing, mocking His pretensions, determined that He would not betray me into Negroness. If there lingered still in the deep recesses of my real self some consciousness of a religious spirit, then the ideal self—the Negro-hating me—did all it could to exorcise it.

How unmitigating and long-lasting this conflict was is proved for me in the fact that only in the last ten years have I been able to go to church without a feeling of indulging in some senseless necromantic ritual, and without feeling that my wanting to go—and I did many times *want* to go; if this seems contradictory, I cannot help it—was a mark of inferiority, the foolish expression of a weak and senseless wish to attain an impossible realm of being differing in its essential nature—that is, in its reality—from anything my experience has taught me can be attained. I do not believe in an afterlife; in otherworldliness. The experiences of this world are too potent and too much with me. I do not see how any Negro can believe in another world, and the religion which has inspired him to that belief, if it has saved him, has done so by making him content with the very degradation of his humanity that is so abhorrent to the principles of Christianity.

But it is not alone for the reasons outlined above that I have held religion suspect. Let us concede that the God of the Negroes has been largely a pagan god and largely stripped of the divinest attributes, interceding intimately and directly for man without man's help. They have fashioned a god to their need. But the whites also have fashioned a god to their need, and have believed in him, and have professed to follow him. He is a moral God, a God of truth and justice and love. I do not wish to carry this too far, for I have no capacity for philosophic speculation; but it seems to me that if the qualities attributed to God represent man's acknowledged needs, and if the principles of Christianity represent the universal source of man's social genius, then he has sacrificed the fulfillment of his basic needs (or "the good life") to the fulfillment of desires that run counter to the purpose of living. He has not given his religion a chance to help him effect that far-going social transformation and evolution which should be religion's end. Religion has become a disembodied sort of activity, when, to be effective, it should be a social function intimately linked up with man's fate on earth.

While there is almost no religion operating in race relations, there is plenty of God. I do not say this facetiously, nor with ironic intent; and, anyway, it has at least been implied before. There is an extensive literature on the part God has played in race relations since the fifteenth century. Principally God and the word of God have been used to perpetuate the wicked idea of human inferiority. I need not go into this farther than to point out modern man's subtle modifications of the idea of God and the intellectual gymnastics that have made those modifications possible, even when, it seems to me, the environment has not made them necessary, and even though in the fundamental concept of the Godhead is the idea of immutability. But God has changed, and though man himself has wrought these changes, he has declared them God's own changes and therefore factors, equations, and of a piece with the mysterious and unknowable nature of God. Indeed, God's very supernaturalness, His mysteriousness and inscrutability ("God moves in mysterious ways His wonders to perform," *ergo* "we cannot know God's purpose in making the black race inferior to the white," and we cannot "fathom the repulsion which God has given one race for another, or one people for another") are largely modern attributions which confound the ancient knowledge and excuse modern sin. God was not always so.

And before the ancient concepts crashed under the onslaught of sophistication, of scientific materialism and the new philosophies it brought into being, Christianity had become a way of life. It had become a way of life to be striven for because it seemed to satisfy the needs of ordinary men. There is nothing mysterious about Christianity. Granted that mystery reposes in the life of Christ (as, let it be said, it did not originally repose in God)—but Christ's life and what he is reported to have done are one thing: what he is reported to have taught is another. What he taught is as clear and concrete and literal as the lead story in a good newspaper. He taught that the kingdom of heaven is here on earth. He preached that men should love one another. He said that all men are brothers. He sought to bind men together in one mighty neighborhood. He was, for all the mystery surrounding him, a social engineer with a far and cosmic vision. The present age has not denied that he was right. Though there are those (and I among them) who reject the traditionally perpetuated events of his life as a factual record, his ministry remains the source of Christian religion. What has happened is that the age, while acknowledging Christianity as the highest way of life that man has thus far conceived, has denied the authority of God to make man live up to Christ's teachings. The dream of God and the reality of Christ have become separated.

If all this seems oversimplified, then I must again plead my lack of resources for such speculation. I do not wish to give an appearance of simplicity to problems that have taxed the best religious philosophers of the past six hundred years. Theology quite aside, it seems to me that the bearing which the Christian religion should have on human relations throughout the world and on race relations in the Western world is simple enough and direct enough. Perhaps it sounds somewhat effete to say now, as William James said at the turn of the century, that life becomes tiresome and meaningless unless it is constantly refreshed by "communion with a wider self through which saving experiences come," but this seems to me to be true. The Christian religion offers that communion with "a wider self." It offers a mature approach to experience. Modern man's incredible good luck in escaping the direst consequences of conduct unlighted by luminous beliefs and uncontrolled by moral principles is fast running out. A third world war may destroy man altogether—if, that is, he does not destroy himself in more subtle and tortuous ways without war. It would be foolish optimism not to assume the possibility of this.

It is not the nobility of Christ's life that I would urge; it is the practicality of his injunctions. It is more a matter of being sensible than of being "good." What I would see joined is the battle between reason and superstition, progress and prejudice, order and chaos, survival and destruction.

17

NOW THAT I COME TO THE END OF
this essay I realize that I have not done for myself
all that I had hoped to do. I am not purged: I am not
cured of my sickness. Perhaps it is not of the sort that
can be cured by individual home remedies. I thought
that in the writing of the essay I could pour myself out, in the manner of a Job or a Jeremiah, or
through a kind of free recall achieve the liberation
and inner peace which seemed so desirable. But even
as I wrote I discovered that the very fact of being Negro limited the freedom to pour myself out. I discovered depths of self-consciousness and facets of experience that I simply could not expose and that gave me
feelings of shame to recognize as my own. Not to
write out these things was cowardly, of course, but no
man can tell the whole truth about himself, and
the charge of cowardice is easier to take than the
traditional, detrusive charges of "Negro" insensitivity,
emotionalism, abandonment and self-pity. Moreover,
what I had to say about myself, if it made me appear
bad and unprincipled, would be taken as typical of
the whole Negro race, and I found myself being very
conscious of this as I wrote. I doubt that race-con-
sciousness operates in this way in the work of white
writers.

I like to think that I made a clear choice between

telling the whole truth and thus saving myself (which was my avowed original intent) and not telling the whole truth and thus protecting the Negro race against the prejudiced opinions which the whole truth would generate. But I know this is pure rationalization. What I have done in this regard was not the result of voluntary decision; it was, rather, evidence of the relentless warping by a neurotic web of coercions, by the need to feel responsible, by the need to have, even disingenuously and even though limited, a sense of belonging and integration.

I have never wanted to be free of this need. I have never wanted to be isolated or alienated, for my belief is that a commitment to something outside oneself is necessary to human and humanistic development. I expressed it long ago in another way: "I did not want sanctuary," I wrote, "a soft nest protected from the hard, strengthening winds that blow hot and cold through the world's teeming, turbulent valley. I wanted to face the wind. I wanted the strength to face it to come from some inexpressibly deep well of feeling of oneness with the wind, of belonging to something, some soul-force outside myself, bigger than myself, but yet a part of me. Not family merely, or institution, or race; but a people and all their topless strivings; a nation and its million destinies." *

What I wanted (and still want—for the writing of this essay has not done it) was to loose and shake off the confining coils of race and the racial experience so that the integration—my personal integration and commitment—can be made to something bigger than race, and more enduring, and truer. For race is a myth: it is artificial; and it is, I hope, at last a dying concept. Meantime, while it lives, it is also a barrier and a terrible, terrible burden. It is a barrier to nearly

* J. Saunders Redding, *No Day of Triumph* (New York: Harper & Brothers, 1942), p. 43. Reprinted by permission of the publisher.

everyone, white and black, in America. It is a burden to everyone too, but it is a personal burden to the Negro—a burden of shame and outrage imposed on him at the earliest moment of consciousness and never lifted till death, and all his energies, mental, emotional, spiritual, must be held in reserve for carrying it.

Though I could not tell it, I saw the whole truth plain, and I think perhaps this seeing helped at least to rid me of the illusion (temporary at best) that there is something ennobling in being able to step aside from the struggle race imposes, and that I would find inner security in doing so. It was a pretty and an attractive illusion. If only I were not Negro!—that, of course, was the impossible dream-wish on which the illusion was founded. But I know now that there is no neutrality in being white in America, and I have at least the comfort of knowing that some white people too suffer from the limitations and frustrations of "whiteness." This was brought home to me more forcefully than ever since I began this essay. This was the meaning, really, of a newspaper story datelined "Brundidge, Ala., June 21 (1951)": "An angry, armed band of white farmers shot a Negro field worker today on the false rumor that he had kidnapped a white woman. Forrest Jones . . . was wounded . . . by a shotgun blast as he returned home after taking a white child, hurt in an automobile accident, to a doctor's office."

A burden on the conscience and on the soul! This is what the books by both Southern apologists and liberals mean. This is what Lillian Smith and Hodding Carter and Howard Odum mean. I can even believe that John Rankin and Richard Russell and James Byrnes and Strom Thurmond signify this in their acts and in their words, and that Theodore Bilbo signified this too. Whiteness does not mitigate the relentless warping by the race situation in America. White men are half-men too—sick men, and perhaps some of them the more to be pitied because they do not know that they are sick. Some of them—the good, lucky ones, like Lillian Smith—have succeeded somewhat in objectifying it; but neither for them nor for me is there a neutral ground on which to stand. Neither they nor I can resign from the human race. The best I can hope to do is to externalize the struggle and set it in the un-confined context of the universal struggle for human dignity and wholeness and unity.

I must confess that, unless I have implied them all along (and this unconsciously), I have no specific remedies for our American sickness. I cannot say that education, in the formal sense, will cure us. Education has failed and has become tiresome in its failures. Or perhaps it is only that prejudice and superstition have opposed any serious attempt to apply education as a remedy. Even though our reason, thoroughly grounded in the scientific knowledge in which the age takes so much pride, backs the ethic of universal brotherhood and declares that "man is a social being who can reach his fullest development only through interaction with his fellows," prejudice and superstition, as the case confirms, are stronger. Prejudice, Lillian Smith points out, declares that there are " 'sacred and profane' people according to criteria as infantile as skin color and as primitive as 'blood,' " and that there must be no interaction between them. Superstition dissociates the fulfillment of man's destiny from man's character, thereby proclaiming that the destiny of society is unknowable and entirely out of the hands of man.

I cannot believe that laws and government are specifics. They are and should be involved with the relationship of the individual to the group, but they are involved only on a superficial level. Laws and government, when controlled by the wrong men—

even a minority of the wrong men—as they frequently are in a democracy, can be perverted. Laws and government discipline, as Talleyrand, I think it was, said, by negatives. They say what cannot be done, but do not necessarily encourage what should be done. They are soulless. Without them, of course, we would have anarchy; but experience does not encourage one to believe that with more laws and government we would have peace. Moreover, they can be set at defiance, and the defiers can often attain renown and rank as courageous patriots.

I would say that Christianity promises a cure for our American sickness. But it must be made truly a way of life in which the dignity and brotherhood of man is the first principle. Perhaps it should be divorced from mysticism and otherworldliness—from theology. I would emphasize the relation of man to man rather than the relation of man to God. I would substitute the authority of Christ's insight for the authority of all ecclesiastical dogma. I would blazon across the earth: "Love ye one another."

THE END